"Luke..." She echoed his name softly, and a warning curled through him at the sound of her soft voice.

He had to keep his distance. This was probably a huge mistake. But where would they go if he denied her the job? What were they running from? He wanted to know everything, but knew that asking would only mean getting closer. And getting close—to anyone—was not an option. Not for him.

He was already in over his head. The fields and the barns were the place for him, and he would let Emily Northcott sort out her own family. She could just get on with doing her job.

He had enough to handle with his own.

Dear Reader

Before I was blessed to turn writing stories into a career, I was a stay-at-home mom. It has been the toughest—and best—job I've ever had. I have never regretted having those precious years at home. And I am very fortunate to have a husband who supported me one hundred percent.

But every now and then I wondered—what would happen if suddenly I was left to provide for our children on my own? I was employed before they were born, but how difficult would it be to get back into the workforce, make ends meet, and still be there for them in the way I wanted? That's exactly what happens to Emily in A FAMILY FOR THE RUGGED RANCHER. I like Emily. Yes, she's been hurt, but she's pulled up her socks to do what's best for her son. She's a good mother. She does what I hope I would have done if I'd found myself in those circumstances. Cope—with a smile.

Of course Luke is dealing with his own issues, and one many of us face as time ticks on: aging parents. He needs someone to bring him out of his shell. To show him all the rich possibilities of the future. And that someone is Emily.

I often hear people say that romance novels are unrealistic fairy tales, but I don't agree. My characters aren't just characters—they're people trying to deal with issues we all face in our lives. And when life gets bad sometimes it's nice to know—just for a while—that the sun is going to peek from beneath that cloud. I'm here to say that fairy tales happen. There *are* such things as happy endings.

I hope you find your happy ending too!

Warm wishes

Donna

A FAMILY
FOR THE
RUGGED RANCHER

BY
DONNA ALWARD

First published in Great Britain 2011
by Mills & Boon, an imprint of Harlequin (UK) Limited,
Eton House, 18-24 Paradise Road, Richmond, Surrey TW9 1SR

© Donna Alward 2011

ISBN: 978 0 263 22030 8

Harlequin (UK) policy is to use papers that are natural, renewable
and recyclable products and made from wood grown in sustainable
forests. The logging and manufacturing process conform to the
legal environmental regulations of the country of origin.

Printed and bound in Great Britain
by CPI Antony Rowe, Chippenham, Wiltshire

A busy wife and mother of three (two daughters and the family dog), **Donna Alward** believes hers is the best job in the world: a combination of stay-at-home mum and romance novelist. An avid reader since childhood, Donna always made up her own stories. She completed her Arts Degree in English Literature in 1994, but it wasn't until 2001 that she penned her first full-length novel and found herself hooked on writing romance. In 2006 she sold her first manuscript, and now writes warm, emotional stories for Harlequin Mills & Boon's Cherish line.

In her new home office in Nova Scotia, Donna loves being back on the east coast of Canada after nearly twelve years in Alberta, where her career began, writing about cowboys and the west. Donna's debut Romance, HIRED BY THE COWBOY, was awarded the Booksellers Best Award in 2008 for Best Traditional Romance.

With the Atlantic Ocean only minutes from her doorstep, Donna has found a fresh take on life and promises even more great romances in the near future!

Donna loves to hear from readers. You can contact her through her website at www.donnaalward.com, her page at www.myspace.com/dalward, or through her publisher.

A great editor is worth her weight in gold.
To Sally, for her constant faith that I'm up to the task.
It means more than you know.

CHAPTER ONE

"ARE WE HERE, Mama? Is Daddy here?"

Emily smiled, though Sam's innocent question made her heart quiver. Sam looked for Rob everywhere, never giving up hope no matter how often he was disappointed. "Yes," she replied, "we're here. But Daddy's not coming, remember? I'm here to start a brand-new job."

She touched the brake pedal as she entered the farmyard of Evans and Son. It was bigger than she'd imagined, sprawling across several acres criss-crossed with fence lines and dotted with leafy green poplar trees. She slowed as she approached the plain white two-story house that rested at the end of the drive. It was flanked on one side by a gigantic barn and on the other by a large workshop with two oversized garage doors. More outbuildings were interspersed throughout the yard, all of them tidy and well-kept. The grass around them was newly clipped and the bits of peeling paint made for a broken-in look rather than broken-down.

Evans and Son looked to be doing all right in the overall scheme of things—which was more than Emily could say for her family. But she was going to change all that. Starting today.

She parked to the right of the house, inhaling deeply and letting out a slow breath, trying to steady herself. When she looked into the back seat, she saw Sam's eyes opening, taking a moment to focus and realize the vehicle had stopped.

"But I want to see Daddy."

"I know, baby." Emily told herself to be patient, he was only five. "Once we're settled, I'll help you write a letter. Maybe you can draw him a picture. What do you think?"

Sam's eyes still held that trace of confusion and sadness that had the power to hurt Emily more than anything else. Sam had been clingier than usual lately. It was hardly a surprise. She'd put the house up for sale and their things in storage. She'd announced that they were leaving the city, which also meant leaving playschool friends and everything familiar, and a five-year-old couldn't be expected to understand her reasons. But the house in Calgary held too many memories—happy and devastating by turns. Both Emily and Sam were stuck in wishing for the past—a past that was long over. Rob had moved on, withdrawing not only his financial support but, more importantly, severing emotional ties with both of them.

Emily would never understand that, especially where his son was concerned. But now it was time to let go and build a new life. One where they could be happy. One where Emily could support her son and find her own way rather than wishing for what should have been. There was a certain freedom to be found in knowing she could make her own decisions now. Her choices were hers to make and hers alone. A massive responsibility, but a liberating one, too.

She reminded herself that a happier life for the two of them was why she was here. "Wait here for just a moment while I knock on the door, okay? Then we'll get settled, I promise."

"It's quiet here."

"I know." Emily smiled, trying to be encouraging. "But there is still sound. Listen closely, Sam, and when I get back you can tell me what you heard."

Sam had only ever lived in the city, with the sounds of traffic and sirens and voices his usual background music. But Emily remembered what it was like to live outside the metropolitan area, where the morning song wasn't honking horns but birds warbling in the caragana bushes and the shush of the breeze through poplar leaves. For the first time in months, she was starting to feel hope that this was all going to turn out all right.

"Wait here, okay? Let me talk to Mr. Evans first, and then I'll come for you."

"Okay, Mama." Sam reached over and picked up his favorite storybook, the Dr. Seuss one with the tongue twisters that he'd practically memorized. Emily paused, her tender smile wavering just a little. Sometimes Sam seemed to see and understand too much. Had the breakdown of her marriage forced her son to grow up too soon?

"I won't be long, sweetie." Emily blew him a kiss, shut the car door and straightened her T-shirt, smoothing it over the hips of her denim capris. It was really important that everything got off on the right foot, so she practiced smiling, wanting it to seem natural and not show her nervousness. She climbed the few steps to the front porch, gathered her courage and rapped sharply on the door.

No one answered.

This was not a great beginning, and doubts crept in, making her wonder if it was a sign that she was making a big mistake with this whole idea. Selling the house and uprooting the two of them was a bit of a radical move, she knew that. She glanced back at the car only feet away and saw Sam's dark head still bent over his book. No, this was best. Her experience as a mom and homemaker was what made her perfect for this job, she realized. She'd loved being a stay-at-home mom, and being with Sam was the most important thing.

Maybe Mr. Evans simply hadn't heard her. She knocked

again, folding her hands. It was a bit nerve-wracking being hired for a job sight unseen. She'd interviewed at the agency but this was different. She'd have to pass Mr. Evans's tests, too. He had the final say. When was the last time she'd had a real interview? All of her résumés over the last year had been sent out without so much as a nibble in return. No one wanted to hire a lab tech who'd been out of the work force for the past five years.

She forced herself to stay calm, stave off the disappointment she felt as her second knock also went unanswered.

"Can I help you?"

The voice came from her right and her stomach twisted into knots as a man approached from the shop, wiping dirty hands on a rag. This was Mr. Evans? He looked younger than she was, for heaven's sake. He wore faded jeans and dusty roper boots, his long stride eating up the ground between them. His baseball cap shaded his eyes so that she couldn't quite see them. The dark T-shirt he wore was stained with grease, stretched taut over a muscled chest. All in all he had the look of honest work about him. And honest work ranked high on her list of attributes lately, she thought bitterly. Good looks didn't.

"I...I'm Emily Northcott. I'm here from the agency?" She hated how uncertain that sounded, so she amended, "From Maid on Demand."

There was a slight pause in his stride while Emily went back down the steps. They met at the bottom, the grass tickling Emily's toes in her sandals as she held out her hand.

The man held up his right hand. "Luke Evans. I'd better not. You don't want to get grease on your hands."

Embarrassment crept hotly up her cheeks, both because she knew she should have realized his hands would be dirty and because of his flat tone. Emily dropped her hand to her side and tried a smile. "Oh, right. I hope we…I…haven't come at a bad time."

"Just fixing some machinery in the shed. I heard the car pull up. Wasn't expecting you though."

"Didn't the agency call?"

"I'm not often in the house to answer the phone." He stated it as if it were something obvious that she'd missed.

Emily frowned. His communication skills could use some work. Didn't he have a cell phone like most normal people? Or voice mail? Or was he being deliberately difficult?

"I was specifically given today as a start date and directions to your place, Mr. Evans."

He tucked the rag into the back pocket of his jeans. "They probably called my sister. She's the one who placed the ad."

"Your sister?"

"My sister Cait. They might have tried there, but she's in the hospital."

"Oh, I'm sorry. I hope it's nothing serious." His answers were so clipped they merely prompted more questions, but his stance and attitude didn't exactly inspire her to ask them.

Finally he gave in and smiled. Just a little, and it looked like it pained him to do so. But pain or not, the look changed his face completely. The icy blue of his eyes thawed a tad and when he smiled, matching creases formed on either side of his mouth. "Nothing too serious," he replied. "She's having a baby."

The news made his smile contagious and Emily smiled back, then caught herself. She clenched her fingers, nervous all over again. She hadn't really given a thought to age…or to the fact that the rancher looking for a housekeeper might be somewhat attractive. What surprised her most was that she noticed at all. Those thoughts had no place in her head right now, considering the scars left from her last relationship and her determination not to put herself through that again.

And Evans wasn't a looker, not in a classic turn-your-head handsome sort of way. But there was something about the tilt of his smile, as though he was telling a joke. Or the way that his cornflower-blue eyes seemed to see right into her. He had inordinately pretty eyes for a man, she thought ridiculously. Had she really thought "somewhat" attractive? She swallowed. He was long, lean and muscled, and his voice held a delicious bit of grit. His strength made up for the lack of pretty. More than made up for it.

Suddenly, being a housekeeper to a single man in the middle of nowhere didn't seem like the bright idea it had been a week ago.

"The agency hired me," she repeated.

He let out a short laugh. "So you said."

Emily resisted the urge to close her eyes, wondering if he'd seen clear through to her last thoughts. Maybe the prairie could just open up and swallow her, and save her more embarrassment. "Right."

"You're able to start today?"

Hope surged as she opened her eyes and found him watching her steadily. He wasn't giving her the brush-off straight away after all. "Yes, sir." She forced a smile. "I can start today."

"Mom, can't I come out now? It's hot in here."

The nerves in Emily's stomach froze as Sam's soft voice came from the car. Luke's head swiveled in the direction of the car, and Emily gave in and sighed. Dammit. She hadn't even had a chance to talk to Evans about their arrangements or anything. A muscle ticked in Luke's jaw and he looked back at her, the smile gone now, the edges of his jaw hard and forbidding.

"My son, Sam," she said weakly.

"You have children."

"Child—just Sam. He's five and no trouble, I promise.

Good as gold." That was stretching it a bit; Sam was a typical five-year-old who was as prone to curiosity and frustrations as any child his age. She looked again at Evans and knew she had to convince him. He was the one who'd advertised. She'd gone through the agency screening and they had hired her for the job. If this didn't work out she had nowhere to go. And she wanted to stay here. She'd liked the look of the place straight off.

Another moment and he'd have her begging. She straightened her shoulders. She would not beg. Not ever again. She could always go to her parents. It wasn't what she wanted, and there'd be a fair amount of told-you-so. Her parents had never quite taken to Rob, and the divorce hadn't come as a big surprise to them. It wasn't that they didn't love her or would deny her help. It was just...

She needed to do this herself. To prove to herself she could and to be the parent that Sam deserved. She couldn't rely on other people to make this right. Not even her parents.

"Mrs. Northcott, this is a ranch, not a day care." The smile that had captivated her only moments before had disappeared, making his face a frozen mask. The warm crinkles around his lips and eyes were now frown marks and Emily felt her good intentions go spiraling down the proverbial drain.

"It's Ms.," she pointed out tartly. It wasn't her fault that there'd been a mix-up. "And Sam is five, hardly a toddler who needs following around all the time." She raised an eyebrow. "Mothers have been cleaning and cooking *and* raising children since the beginning of time, Mr. Evans."

She heard the vinegar in her voice and felt badly for speaking so sharply, but she was a package deal and the annoyance that had marked his face when he heard Sam's voice put her back up.

"I'm well aware of that. However, I didn't advertise for a family. I advertised for a housekeeper."

"Your *sister*—" she made sure to point out the distinction "—advertised with Maid on Demand Domestics. If any part of that ad wasn't clear, perhaps you need to speak to them. The agency is aware I have a son, so perhaps there was a flaw with the ad. I interviewed for the job and I got it." She lifted her chin. "Perhaps you would have been better off going without an agency?"

She knew her sharp tongue was probably shooting her chances in the foot, but she couldn't help it. She was hardly to blame. Nor would she be made to feel guilty or be bullied, not anymore. If he didn't want her services, he could just say so.

"It's not that…I tried putting an ad in the paper and around town…oh, why am I explaining this to you?" he asked, shoving his hands into his pockets despite any grease remaining on his fingers.

"If it's that you don't like children…" That would make her decision much easier. She wouldn't make Sam stay in an unfriendly environment. No job was worth that. She backed up a step and felt her hands tightening into anxious fists.

"I didn't say that." His brow wrinkled. He was clearly exasperated.

She caught a hint of desperation in his voice and thought perhaps all wasn't lost. "Then your objection to my son is…"

"Mom!" The impatient call came from the car and Emily gritted her teeth.

"Excuse me just a moment," she muttered, going to the car to speak to Sam.

It was hot inside the car, and Emily figured she had nothing to lose now. "You can get out," she said gently, opening the door. "Sorry I made you wait so long."

"Are we staying here?"

"I'm not sure."

Sam held his mother's hand...something he rarely did any more since he'd started preschool and considered himself a big boy. Perhaps Evans simply needed to meet Sam and talk to him. It had to be harder to say no to children, right? It wasn't Sam's fault his life had been turned upside down. Emily was trying to do the right thing for him. A summer in the country had sounded perfect. This place was new and different with no history, no bad memories. She just needed to show Evans that Sam would be no extra trouble.

"Mr. Evans, this is my son, Sam."

Evans never cracked a smile. "Sam."

"Sir," Sam replied. Emily was vastly proud that Sam lifted his chin the tiniest bit, though his voice was absolutely respectful.

Emily put a hand on Sam's shoulder. "The agency did know about him, Mr. Evans. I'm not trying to pull a fast one here. If it's a deal-breaker, tell me now and take it up with them. But you should know that I'm fully qualified for this job. I know how to cook and clean and garden. I'm not afraid of hard work and you won't be sorry you hired me."

He shook his head, and Emily noticed again the color of his eyes, a brilliant shade of blue that seemed to pierce straight through her. Straightforward, honest eyes. She liked that. Except for the fact that his gaze made her want to straighten her hair or fuss with the hem of her shirt. She did neither.

"I'm sorry," he replied.

That was it, then. Maybe he had a kind side somewhere but it didn't extend to giving her the job. She would not let him see the disappointment sinking through her body to her toes, making the weight of her situation that much heavier to carry. She wouldn't let it matter. She'd bounced back from worse over the last year. She'd find something else.

"I'm sorry I've taken up your time," she said politely. She took Sam's hand and turned back towards her car.

"Where are you going?"

His surprised voice made her halt and turn back. He'd taken off his cap and was now running his hand over his short-clipped hair. It was sandy-brown, she noticed. The same color as his T-shirt.

"I never said the job wasn't yours. I was apologizing."

Is that what that was? Emily wanted to ask but sensed things were at a delicate balance right now and could go either way. She simply nodded, holding her breath.

"The job description said room and board included." She was pushing it, but this had to be settled before either of them agreed to anything. She felt Sam's small hand in hers. She wanted to give him a summer like the ones she remembered. Open spaces and simple pleasures. Some peace and quiet and new adventures rather than the reminders of their once happy life as a whole family. Life wasn't going to be the same again, and Emily didn't know what to do to make it better anymore. And this farm—it was perfect. She could smell the sweet fragrance of lilacs in the air. The lawn was huge, more than big enough for a child to play. She'd glimpsed a garden on the way in, and she imagined showing Sam how to tell weeds from vegetables and picking peas and beans later in the summer when they were plump and ripe.

"I offered room and board, but only for one. Adding an extra is unexpected."

"I'll make sure he doesn't get in your way," she assured him quickly, hearing the edge of desperation in her voice, knowing she was *this* close to hearing him say yes. "And we can adjust my pay if that helps." She wished she weren't so transparent. She didn't want him to know how badly she wanted this to work out. She was willing to compromise. Was he?

Pride warred with want at this moment. She didn't want to tell Luke Evans how much it would mean for them to stay here, but seeing the look of wonder on Sam's face as he spotted a hawk circling above, following its movements until it settled on a fence post, searching for mice or prairie dogs… She'd do anything to keep that going. Even if it meant sacrificing her pride just a little bit.

"Little boys probably don't eat much. If you're sure to keep him out of the way… I have a farm to run, Ms. Northcott."

He put a slight emphasis on the Ms., but she ignored it as excitement rushed through her. He was doing it! He was giving her the job, kid and all. For the first time in five years she would be earning her own money. She was making a first step towards self-reliance, and she'd done it all on her own. Today keeping house for Luke Evans…who knew what the future would hold? She reveled in the feeling of optimism, something that had been gone for a long time. She offered a small smile and wondered what he was thinking. She would make sure he didn't regret it and that Sam would mean little disruption to his house. "You mean we can stay?"

"You're a housekeeper, aren't you? The agency did hire you."

The acid tone was back, so she merely nodded, the curl at her temple flopping.

"And you did say you could cook and clean. I'm counting on it."

She smiled at him then, a new confidence filling her heart. Lordy, he was so stern! But perhaps he could smile once in a while. Maybe she could make him. Right now she felt as though she could do anything.

"Oh, yes. That's definitely not an omission or exaggeration. I've been a stay-at-home mom since Sam was born. I promise you, Mr. Evans, I can clean, cook and do laundry with my eyes closed." She could sew, too, and make origami animals out of plain paper and construct Halloween costumes out of some cardboard, newspaper and string. The latter skills probably weren't a high priority on a ranch.

"Just remember this is a working ranch, not a summer camp. There is a lot of work to be done and a lot of machinery around. Make sure the boy doesn't cause any trouble, or go where he shouldn't be going."

"His name is Sam, and you have my word." She'd watch Sam with eyes in the back of her head if she had to. She had a job. And one where she could still be there for Sam—so important right now as he went through the stress of a family breakup.

"Then bring your things inside. I'll show you around quickly. Bear in mind I was unprepared for you, so none of the rooms are ready. You'll have to do that yourself while I fix the baler."

He was letting them stay. She knew she should just accept it and be grateful, but she also knew it was not what he'd wanted or planned, and she felt compelled to give him one more chance to be sure. "Are you certain? I don't want to put you out, Mr. Evans. It's obvious this is a surprise for you. I don't want you to feel obligated. We can find other accommodation."

He paused. "You need this job, don't you?"

He gave her a pointed look and Emily shifted her gaze to her feet. She added a mental note: not only stern but keenly sharp, too. Yes, she did need the job. Until the money went through from the sale of the house, they were on a shoe-string and even then their circumstances would be drastically changed. It was why they'd had to sell in the first place. With no money coming in and Rob neglecting to pay child support, the savings account had dried up quickly and she couldn't afford to make the mortgage payments. She couldn't hide the frayed straps of her sandals and the older model, no-frills vehicle she drove instead of the luxury sedan she'd traded in six months ago. Everything was different. It wasn't the hardest thing about the divorce, but after a while a woman couldn't ignore practicalities.

He took her silence as assent. "And I need someone to look after the house. It doesn't make sense for you to pay to stay somewhere else, and days are long here. The deal was room and board, so that's what you'll get. How much trouble can one boy be, anyway?"

CHAPTER TWO

LUKE TRIED TO keep his body relaxed as he held open the screen door, but Emily Northcott was making it difficult. Whatever she had put on for perfume that morning teased his nostrils. It was light and pretty, just like her. Her short hair was the color of mink and curled haphazardly around her face, like the hair cover models had that was meant to look deliberately casual. And she had the biggest brown eyes he'd ever seen, fringed with thick dark lashes.

When he'd first advertised for a housekeeper, Emily was not what he'd had in mind. He'd figured on someone local, someone, well, *older* to answer his ad. A motherly figure with graying hair, definitely not someone who looked like Emily. Someone who lived nearby who could arrive in the morning and leave again at dinnertime. But when his local ads had gone unanswered week after week, he'd put Cait on the job. She'd been getting so clucky and meddling as her pregnancy progressed. He'd thought it would be a good project for her and would keep her out of his hair. It was only the promise of getting outside help that had ceased her constant baking and fussing over the house. Not that he didn't need the help. He did, desperately. But having Cait underfoot all the time had been driving him crazy.

Maid on Demand had seemed like the perfect solution, anonymous and impersonal. Except now he'd ended up worse off than ever—with a beautiful woman with a family of her own, 24/7.

He should have said no, flat-out.

He'd be a bald-faced liar if he said Emily Northcott wasn't the prettiest woman to pass through his door in months. Just the scent of her put him on alert. Not that he was in the market for a girlfriend. But he was human, after all.

But what could he say? No, you can't stay because you're too pretty? Because you're too young? She couldn't be more than thirty. And then there was her son. How could he turn her away for that reason either? He'd have to be cold-hearted to use that against her. So far the boy had hardly made a peep. And it was only for a few months, after all. Once things wound down later in the fall, he'd be better able to handle things on his own.

"Have a look around," he suggested, as the screen door slapped shut behind them. "I'm going to wash up. I've had my hands inside the baler for the better part of the afternoon. Then I'll give you the nickel tour."

He left her standing in the entry hall while he went to the kitchen and turned on the tap. The whole idea of hiring help was to make his summer easier, not add more responsibility to it. But that was exactly how it felt. If she stayed, it meant two extra bodies to provide for over the next few months. Twice as many mouths to feed than he'd expected. And having that sort of responsibility—whether real or implied—was something he never wanted to do again. He liked his life plain, simple and uncomplicated. Or at least as uncomplicated as it could be considering his family circumstances.

He scrubbed the grease from his hands with the pumice paste, taking a nail brush and relentlessly applying it to his nails. The plain truth was that not one soul had applied for the job—not even a teenager looking for summer work. Cait had put the listing with the agency nearly three weeks ago.

Things were in full swing now and he needed the help. Luke was already working sun-up to sundown. The housework was falling behind, and he was tired of eating a dry sandwich when he came in at the end of the day. He was barely keeping up with the laundry, putting a load in when he was falling-down tired at night.

They could stay as long as it meant they stayed out of his way. He didn't have time for babysitting along with everything else.

When he returned from the kitchen, Emily was in the living room on the right, her fingertips running over the top of an old radio and record player that had long ceased to work and that now held a selection of family photos on its wooden cover. His heart contracted briefly, seeing her gentle hands on the heirloom, but he pushed the feeling aside and cleared his throat. "You ready?"

"This is beautiful. And very old."

He nodded. "It was my grandparents'. They used to play records on it. Some of the LPs are still inside, but the player doesn't work anymore."

"And this is your family?"

Luke stepped forward and looked at the assortment of photos. There were three graduation pictures—him and his sisters when they'd each completed twelfth grade. Cait's and Liz's wedding pictures were there as well, and baby pictures of Liz's children. Soon Cait's new baby would be featured there, too. There was a picture of three children all together, taken one golden autumn several years earlier, and in the middle sat a picture of his parents, his dad sitting down and his mom's hand on his shoulder as they smiled for the camera. The last two pictures were difficult to look at. That had been the year that everything had changed. First his mom, and then his dad.

"My sister's doing. Our parents always had pictures on here and she keeps it stocked."

He saw a wrinkle form between her eyebrows and his jaw tightened. He wasn't all that fond of the gallery of reminders, but Cait had insisted. He'd never been able to deny her anything, and he knew to take the pictures down would mean hurting Cait, and Liz, too, and he couldn't do it.

"Your dad looks very handsome. You look like him. In the jaw and the shape of your mouth."

Luke swallowed. He could correct her, but he knew in reality the handsome bit no longer applied to his father. Time and illness had leached it from his body, bit by painful bit. Luke didn't want to be like him. Not that way. Not ever. The fact that he might not have a choice was something he dealt with every single day.

"I have work to do, Ms. Northcott. Do you think we can continue the tour now?"

She turned away from the family gallery and smiled at him. He'd done his best not to encourage friendliness, so why on earth was she beaming at him? It was like a ray of sunshine warming the room when she smiled at him like that. "I'd love to," she replied.

Luke didn't answer, just turned away from the radio with a coldness that he could see succeeded in wiping the smile from her face. "Let's get a move on, then," he said over his shoulder. "So I can get back to work."

Emily scowled at his departing back. She had her work cut out for her, then. To her mind, Luke Evans had lived alone too long. His interpersonal skills certainly needed some polishing. Granted, her life hadn't been all sunshine and flowers lately, but she at least could be pleasant. She refused to let his sour attitude ruin her day.

"Do you mind if I turn the TV on for Sam? That way we

can get through faster. I don't want to hold you up." After his comment about Sam being a distraction, Emily figured this was the easiest way. After Evans was gone to the barn, she'd enlist Sam's help and they'd work together. Make it fun.

As they started up the stairs, Luke turned around and paused, his hand on the banister. "I apologize for the sorry state of the house," he said. "My sister hasn't been by in a few weeks and with haying time and the new calves…"

"Isn't that why I'm here?"

"I don't want to scare you off," he said, starting up the stairs once more. Gruff or not, Emily got the feeling that he was relieved she was there. Or at least relieved *someone* was there to do the job he required.

She followed him up, unable to avoid the sight of his bottom in the faded jeans. Two identical wear spots lightened the pockets. As he took her through the house she realized he hadn't been exaggerating. The spare rooms had a fine film of dust on the furniture. The rugs were in desperate need of a vacuuming and he'd left his shaving gear and towel on the bathroom vanity this morning, along with whiskers dotting the white porcelain of the sink. The linen closet was a jumbled mess of pillows, blankets and sheets arranged in no particular order, and the laundry basket was filled to overflowing.

The tour continued and Emily tried to be positive through it all. "The floors are gorgeous," she tried, hoping to put them on more of an even footing. "They look like the original hardwood."

"They are. And they have the scratches to prove it."

She bit back a sigh and tried again. "Scratches just add character. And the doors are solid wood rather than those hollow imitations in stores these days. Such a great color of stain."

"They need refinishing."

Emily gave up for the time being; her attempts at anything

positive were completely ineffectual. She simply followed him
down the hall. The smallest bedroom was painted a pale green
and had one wall on a slant with a charming oval window
looking over the fields. She fell in love with it immediately.
A second room was painted pink and one wall had rosebud
wallpaper. A third door remained closed—she presumed it
was his room. But when he opened the door to the final room
she caught her breath. It must have been his parents' room, all
gleaming dark wood and an ivory chenille spread. It was like
stepping back in time—hooked rugs on the floor and dainty
Priscilla curtains at the windows.

"What a beautiful room." She looked up at Luke and saw
a muscle tick in his jaw. It was almost as if seeing it caused
him pain, but why?

"It belonged to my parents," he answered, and shut the door
before she could say any more.

Back in the kitchen the clean dishes were piled in the
drying rack, the teetering pile a masterpiece of domestic en-
gineering. In the partner sink, dirty dishes formed a smaller,
stickier pile. The kitchen cupboards were sturdy solid oak,
and Emily knew a washing with oil soap would make them
gleam again. The fridge needed a good wiping down. She
paused a moment to glance at the magnetic notepad stuck to
the fridge door. It was simply a list of phone numbers. She
frowned as she read the names *Cait* and *Liz,* wondering why
he didn't simply have his sister's numbers memorized. After
his brusqueness, there was no way on earth she'd ask.

Overall, the house was a throwback to what felt like a happier, simpler time. "All it needs is some love and polish, Mr.
Evans. You have a beautiful home."

The tour finished, Luke cleared his throat, his feet shift-
ing from side to side. "I really need to get back to fixing the
baler. This weather isn't going to hold and I have help coming
tomorrow. The job is yours, Ms. Northcott."

She grinned at him, ready to tackle the dust and cobwebs and bring the house back to its former glory "You've got a deal."

"Shouldn't we talk salary?"

A shadow dimmed her excitement, but only for a moment. "I thought that was all taken care of through the agency. Unless you've made a change regarding..." She paused, glancing down at Sam.

"One boy won't eat much. The wage stands, if it's acceptable to you."

"Agreed."

"You'll be okay to get settled then?"

"Oh, we'll be fine. Does it matter which rooms we take?"

"One of the two smaller ones at the end of the hall would probably be best for your son," he replied. "My sister Liz's pink room probably wouldn't suit him. The other is still a bit girly, but at least it's not pink. You can take the one on the other side." The master bedroom, the one that had been his parents.

"Are you sure you don't want me to take the pink room? The other is..." she paused. She remembered the look on his face when he'd opened the door, but had no idea how to ask why it hurt him so much. "The other is so big," she said.

Luke tried not to think of Emily in his parents' room, covered with the ivory chenille spread that had been on the bed as long as he could remember. He had never been able to bring himself to change rooms, instead staying in the one he'd had since childhood. Nor did he want Sam there. But Emily...somehow she fit. She'd be caring and respectful.

"The room has been empty a long time. You may as well use it. The other is so small. It's just a room, Emily. No reason why you shouldn't sleep in it."

But it wasn't "just a room", and as he looked down into her

dark gaze, he got the idea she understood even without the details.

"Mr. Evans, I don't know how to thank you. This means a lot to me...to us."

Her eyes were so earnest, and he wondered what was behind them. Clearly she was a single mom and things had to be bad if she accepted a short-term position like his and was so obviously happy about it. She hadn't even attempted to negotiate salary.

"What brought you here? I mean...you're obviously a single mother." No husband to be found and insistent on the Ms. instead of Mrs. No wedding ring either, but he saw the slight indentation on her finger where one had lived. "Recently divorced?"

The pleasant smile he'd enjoyed suddenly disappeared from her mouth. "Does it matter if I'm divorced?"

He stepped back. "Not at all. I was just curious."

"You don't strike me as the curious type."

He hoped he didn't blush. She had him dead to rights and she knew it. He had always been the stay-out-of-others'-business-and-they'll-stay-out-of-yours type.

"Pardon me," he replied coolly.

But her lack of answers only served to make him wonder more what had truly brought her here. What circumstances had led Emily Northcott and her son to his doorstep?

"Yes," she relented, "I'm divorced. Sam's father is living in British Columbia. I'm just trying to make a living and raise my son, Mr. Evans."

She was a mom. She had baggage, if the white line around her finger and the set of her lips were any indication. It all screamed *off limits* to him. He should just nod and be on his way. Instead he found himself holding out his hand, scrubbed clean of the earlier grease, with only a telltale smidge remaining in his cuticles.

"Luke. Call me Luke."

The air in the room seemed to hold for a fraction of a second as she slid her hand out of her pocket and towards his. Then he folded the slim fingers within his, the connection hitting him square in the gut. Two dots of color appeared on Emily's cheeks, and it looked as though she bit the inside of her lip.

Not just him then. As if things weren't complicated enough.

"Luke," she echoed softly, and a warning curled through him at the sound of her voice. He had to keep his distance. This was probably a huge mistake. But where would they go if he denied her the job? What were they running from? He wanted to know everything but knew that asking would only mean getting closer. And getting close—to anyone—was not an option. Not for him.

He was already in over his head. The fields and barns were the place for him, and he would let Emily Northcott sort out her own family. She could just get on with doing her job.

He had enough to handle with his own.

CHAPTER THREE

THE REST OF the day passed in a blur. Emily began her cleaning upstairs in the rooms that she and Sam would occupy. Sam helped as best as a five-year-old boy could, helping change the sheets, dusting and Emily put him to work putting his clothes in the empty dresser while she moved on to her room. It was late afternoon when she was done and continued on to the kitchen, putting the dry dishes away before tackling the new dirty ones and searching the freezer for something to make for supper. The baked pork chops, rice and vegetables were ready for six o'clock; she held the meal until six-thirty and finally ate with Sam while Luke remained conspicuously absent. It wasn't until she and Sam were picking at the blueberry cobbler she'd baked for dessert that Luke returned.

He took one look at the dirty supper dishes and his face hardened.

Emily clenched her teeth. What did he expect? They couldn't wait all night, and she'd held it as long as was prudent. As it was, the vegetables had been a little mushy and the cream of mushroom sauce on the chops had baked down too far.

"We didn't know how long you'd be," she said quietly, getting up to move the dirty dishes and to fix Luke a plate. "We decided to go ahead."

"You didn't need to wait for me at all." He went to the sink to wash his hands.

Emily bit the inside of her lip. Granted, dinnertime with the surly Luke Evans wasn't all that appealing, but it seemed rude to discount having a civil meal together at all. Still she was new here and the last thing she wanted was to get off on the wrong foot. She picked up a clean plate, filled it with food and popped it into the microwave. In her peripheral vision she could see Sam picking at his cobbler, staring into his bowl. He could sense the tension, and it made Emily even more annoyed. He'd had enough of that when things had got bad between her and Rob. The last thing she wanted was to have him in a less-than-friendly situation again.

"Eating together is a civil thing to do," she replied as the microwave beeped. "Plus the food is best when it's fresh and hot."

"You don't need to go to any bother," he replied, taking the plate and sitting down at the table. Sam's gaze darted up and then down again. Was he not even going to acknowledge her son?

Perhaps what Luke Evans needed was a refresher course in manners and common courtesy.

She resumed her seat, picked up her fork and calmly said, "I wasn't planning on running a short-order kitchen."

"I didn't realize I was nailed down to a specific dinner time. I am running a farm here, you know."

Sam's eyes were wide and he held his spoon with a purple puddle of blueberries halfway between the bowl and his mouth. Emily spared him a glance and let out a slow breath.

"Of course you are, and I did hold the meal for over half an hour. Maybe we should have simply communicated it better. Set a basic time and if you're going to be later, you can let me know."

"I'm not used to a schedule."

Emily looked at Sam and smiled. "You're excused, Sam. Why don't you go upstairs and put on your pajamas?"

Obediently Sam pushed out his chair and headed for the stairs.

Luke paused in his eating. "He listens to you well."

Now that Sam was gone Emily wasn't feeling so generous. "He has been taught some manners," she replied, the earlier softness gone from her voice. "Eating together is the civilized thing to do. Respecting that I may have gone to the trouble to cook a nice meal would go a long way. And acknowledging my son when you sit at the table would be polite, rather than acting as though he doesn't exist."

Luke's fork hit his plate. "I hired you to be a housekeeper, not Miss Manners."

"I'm big on courtesy and respect, Mr. Evans. No matter who or what the age. If you don't want to eat with us, say so now. I'll plan for Sam and I to eat by ourselves and you can reheat your meal whenever it suits you. But I'd prefer if we settled it now so we don't have any more confusion."

For several seconds the dining room was quiet, and then Luke replied, "As long as you understand there may be times when I'm in the middle of something, I will make every attempt to observe a regular dinner hour."

"I appreciate it."

"And I didn't mean to ignore your son."

"He has feelings, too, Mr. Evans. And since his father left, it is easy for him to feel slighted."

Luke picked at the mound of rice on his plate. "I didn't think of that."

"You don't know us yet," Emily responded, feeling her annoyance drain away. Luke looked suitably chastised, and she couldn't help the smile that she tried to hide. She'd seen that look on Sam's face on occasion, and it melted her anger.

"Look, I put in an effort for our first dinner here. I might have gotten a bit annoyed that you weren't here to eat it."

Luke lifted his head and met her eyes. Her heart did a weird thump, twisting and then settling down to a slightly faster rhythm, it seemed.

"I have lived alone a long time," he admitted. "I'm sorry I didn't think of it. You might need to be patient with me."

"Maybe we all need to be patient," she replied, and he smiled at her. A genuine smile, not the tense tight one from this afternoon. The twist in her heart went for another leap again and she swallowed.

"There's cobbler," she said, a peace offering.

"Thank you, Emily," he answered.

She went to the kitchen to get it, hearing the way he said her name echoing around in her brain. She'd fought her battle and won. So why did she feel as if she was in a lot of trouble?

After the supper mess was cleaned up, Luke went out to the barns and Emily put Sam to bed, following him in short order. She was exhausted. She vaguely heard the phone ringing once, but Luke answered it and the sound of the peepers and the breeze through the window lulled her back to sleep.

But the early night meant early to rise, and Emily heard Luke get up as the first pale streaks of sunlight filtered through the curtains. The floorboards creaked by the stairs and she checked her watch…did people really get up this early? She crept out of bed and tiptoed down the hall, looking in on Sam.

He looked so much younger—more innocent, if that were possible—in slumber. He wasn't a baby any longer, but it didn't change the tender feeling that rushed through her looking at his dark eyelashes and curls. He was so good, so loving. So trusting. She didn't want what had happened with his father to change that about him. It was up to her to make sure he had a good life. A happy life. She was determined. He would never doubt how much she loved him. He would always know that she would be there for him.

Back in her room, she slid into a pair of jeans and a T-shirt, moving as quietly as possible. She wanted to get an early start. Make a decent breakfast and get a load of laundry going so she could hang it out on the clothesline. The very idea was exciting, and she laughed a little at herself. Who knew something as simple as fresh-smelling clothes off the line would give her such pleasure? Despite Luke's reticence, despite getting off on the wrong foot last night at dinner, she was more convinced than ever that she'd done the right thing. She'd taken him on and he hadn't given her the boot. She'd be the best housekeeper Luke Evans ever had. And when she got her feet beneath her, it would be time to start thinking about the future.

She was beating pancake batter in a bowl when Luke returned from the barn, leaving his boots on the mat and coming into the kitchen in his stocking feet. Emily had found a cast-iron pan and it was already heating on the burner. He stopped and stared at her for a moment, long enough that she began to feel uncomfortable and her spoon moved even faster through the milky batter.

"I didn't think you'd be up yet."

"I heard you leave a while ago. I wanted to get an early start." She dropped a little butter in the pan and ladled a perfectly round pancake in the middle of it. "You're just in time for the first pancakes." She was glad he was here. Now he'd get them fresh and hot from the pan, better proof of her cooking abilities than the reheated dinner of last evening. She wasn't opposed to hard work, and it felt good having a purpose, something to do. It was just a taste of how it would feel when she got a permanent job and could provide for herself and for Sam.

"Lately I've been grabbing a bowl of cereal. Pancakes are a treat. Thank you, Emily."

His polite words nearly made her blush as she remembered how she'd taken him to task for his manners at their last meal. She focused on turning the pancake, the top perfectly golden brown. "I'm glad you get to enjoy them fresh, rather than warmed up, like last night's supper." She flipped the pancake onto a plate and began frying another. "Besides, when you sleep in you miss the best part of the day, I think."

She wanted to ask him if this was his regular breakfast time but held back, not wanting to harp on a dead topic. Still, she felt as if she should already know, which was ridiculous. How could she possibly know his routine, his preferences?

Everything about Luke Evans was throwing her off balance and she was having to think and double-think every time she wanted to ask him something, measure her words, trying hard to say the right thing and not the first thing that came to her mind.

"What time do you want lunch?"

"I'm used to just grabbing a sandwich when I come in."

She put down the spatula. "A sandwich? But a working man can't live on a sandwich for lunch!"

He laughed then, a real laugh aimed at her open-mouthed look of dismay, she realized. She picked up the spatula again, trying to ignore the light that kindled in his eyes as he laughed. When Luke was grumpy, she wished he were nicer. But when he was nice, something inside her responded and she wished for his sterner side again. She didn't want to have those sorts of reactions. She wasn't interested in romance or flirting. She didn't know how, not after so many years with one man. She was never going to put herself in a position to be hurt like that again either. She deserved more. So did Sam.

"You're making fun of me."

"You sound like my sisters. They both fuss and flutter. I haven't starved yet, though."

The awkwardness had seemed to fade away between them, but what arose in its place was a different kind of tension. It made her want to hold her breath or glance over and see if he was watching her. She couldn't help it—she did, and he was. His blue gaze was penetrating, and she had the simultaneous thoughts that his eyes were too beautiful for a man and that she wished he still wore his hat so they would be at least a bit shadowed.

She handed him the plate of pancakes, taking care to make sure their fingers never touched. "Fresh from the pan."

"They smell delicious. And about lunch… I try to come in around noon, when the boys take their break. Sometimes when I'm haying I take my lunch with me though. I'll be sure to let you know."

Emily bit her lip and turned back to her pancakes, feeling a warmth spread through her. His tone at the end had held a little hint of teasing, no malice in it at all. She could nearly hear the echo of Rob's angry voice in her head, telling her to stop nagging. She had told herself his leaving had been out of the blue, but things hadn't been right for a while before he left. He had complained about her always trying to tie him down to a schedule. She hadn't. But she'd taken pride in her "job". She loved it when they all sat down together. It had been a bone of contention between them that they didn't eat dinner as a family. Since he'd left she'd made it a point to sit with Sam over dinner and talk about their favorite parts of the day.

But Luke wasn't her family, he was her boss. "It's your house," she said quietly. "I overstepped last night. Whenever you want your meals, I'll make sure they're on the table. That *is* what you pay me for, right?"

"Are you okay?"

"Fine. Why?"

"You got all…meek all of a sudden. If you want something, Emily, just ask. If I don't like it, I'll tell you."

She swallowed. Had she become so used to tiptoeing around Rob that she'd forgotten how good honesty and straight-talking felt? She took a breath. "Okay. It would be helpful if I knew what time you'd like your meals so I can plan around them."

His chair scraped against the floor as he rose, came forward and reached around her for the maple syrup. His body was close—too close. When she sucked in a breath, she smelled the clean scent of his soap mixed with a hint of leather and horses. Oh, my. Heat crept into her cheeks.

"Was that so hard?" he asked.

Her brain scrambled to remember what they'd been talking about. Oh, yes. The timing of meals. "Um…no?"

He retrieved the syrup and moved away while Emily wilted against the counter.

"I'll try to let you know when I plan to be in," he said, pouring syrup over his pancakes. "You were right, so don't apologize. It's just business courtesy, that's all." Luke dismissed it with a wave and picked up his fork.

Just business. He was right, and Emily felt chagrined at her earlier behavior. She was far too aware of him and he was her boss. Why shouldn't she simply ask questions? She would of any other employer.

"I have to run into town this morning to pick up a part for the baler. I'll make a stop at the hospital, too, I guess. Cait and Joe had a baby girl last night. Anyway, if there's anything you need, I can get it while I'm there."

A baby! He said it as blandly as he might have said *Rain is forecast for today,* and it left Emily confused. What was she missing? She remembered the first moments of holding Sam in her arms after his birth, and despite Luke's tepid response she

knew his sister and brother-in-law had to be over the moon.
As brother and uncle, he should be, too. "A girl! Lovely! They
must be so happy."

Luke went to the coffeepot and poured himself a cup, then
took down another and held it out, asking her if she wanted
some. She nodded, wondering why he wasn't excited about
the baby. After his reaction to Sam yesterday, she was beginning to think her assessment that he didn't like children was
dead-on. "Is everyone healthy?" she asked, hoping there were
no complications.

"Oh, yes." He gave a shrug. "Another girl. That's four
nieces."

"Do you have something against girls?"

The cup halted halfway to his mouth. "What? Oh, of course
not. We just keep hoping for a boy. To keep the Evans and
Son going, you know?"

Emily watched him as he got out juice glasses—three of
them—pouring orange juice in two and leaving the third one
empty but waiting. He had remembered Sam, then. At times
last night and this morning it had seemed as though Luke
forgot Sam was even there.

"This is the twenty-first century, Luke." She smiled at him,
poured another pancake. "A girl could take over the farm as
well as a boy, you know. Evans and Niece might not have the
same ring to it, but I didn't have you pegged for one worrying about an heir to the empire. Besides, you might still have
some big, strapping prairie boys of your own." She added the
pancake to the stack on the warmer with a smile. But her teasing had backfired. He stared at her now with an expression
that seemed partly hurt and partly angry.

"I don't plan on having a family," he replied, then dropped
his gaze, focusing on cutting his pancakes, his knife scrap-
ing along the porcelain. Emily stared at him for a second,
absolutely nonplussed, and then remembered she still had a

pancake cooking and it needed to be turned if she didn't want it to burn.

He finished the meal in silence as she cooked more pancakes, stacking them until the warmer was full. The quiet stretched out uncomfortably; Emily wanted to break it somehow but after his last words she had no idea what to say that would be a good start to a conversation. He'd clearly ended the last attempt.

He finished what was on his plate and came over to the stove, standing at her elbow. She wished she could ignore him and relax, but he was six foot something of muscled man. She couldn't pretend he didn't exist. Not when all of her senses were clamoring like the bells of a five-alarm fire. She gripped the spatula tightly.

"Are there any more of those, Emily?"

She let her breath out slowly, not wanting him to sense her relief. Extra pancakes—was that all he wanted? "Take as many as you like," she replied. "I can make more for Sam when he gets up."

He lifted four from the warming tray and Emily swallowed against the lump that had formed in her throat. My, he did have a good appetite. Was there nothing about the man that wasn't big and virile? On the back of the thought came the unwanted but automatic comparison to Rob. Rob in his suits and Italian loafers and his fancy car. Rob going out the door with a travel mug and a briefcase in the morning. When those things had disappeared so abruptly from her life it had broken her heart. She'd built her whole life around their little family, loving every moment of caring for their house and watching Sam grow. She'd lost the life she'd always dreamed of and it still hurt.

But it was time to start dreaming about something new. Emily lifted her head and caught a glimpse of the wide fields out the kitchen window. The golden fields were Luke's office.

His jeans and boots and, oh, yes, the T-shirts that displayed his muscled arms were his work clothes. The prairie wind was his air conditioning and the sun his office lighting.

She smiled, knowing that the wide-open space was something she'd been missing for a long time. The memories would always be there, but they hurt less now. As she looked out over the sunny fields, she knew that leaving the city had been the right thing to do. She was moving forward with her life, and it felt good.

"What are you smiling at?" Luke asked the question from the table, but he'd put down his fork and was giving her his full attention. And the pancake batter was gone, leaving her with nothing to do to keep her hands busy. Six pancakes remained; certainly enough for her breakfast with Sam. She put down the bowl and brushed her hands on the apron she'd found in the drawer.

"I was just thinking how nice it must be to go to work in the outdoors," she replied, picking up her cooling coffee. Anything to let her hide just a little bit from Luke's penetrating gaze.

"Not so nice on rainy days, but yeah...I think I'd go crazy locked up inside all day. You strike me as the inside kind."

"What makes you say that?"

He looked down at his tanned arms and then at her pale, white limbs. Then up at her face while a small smile played with his lips.

"Okay, you're right. Sam and I made it to the park but our backyard..." She sighed. "It was very small. Sam had a little slide there, a kid-sized picnic table. That was about it."

"Boys need room to run around."

She poured herself more coffee. "Yes, I know. Suburbia wasn't always part of the plan. I did grow up with more than a postage stamp for a yard, you know. In Regina."

"You're from Regina?"

"Just outside, yes. My mom was a stay-at-home mom and my dad sold cars." Telling Luke took her back to her college days when she'd been slightly ashamed of her modest home and she realized now that Rob had never quite fit in there. Perhaps this split had always been coming, and was not as random as she thought. She'd been trying to be someone she wasn't. Maybe he had, too. Now, despite the fact that she knew there would be a certain bit of "I told you so", home didn't seem so bad. She'd been afraid of being judged, but she knew that wasn't really why she didn't want to go back. She didn't want to go back a failure. She wanted to go back when she could look her parents in the eye and say that she'd fixed it. The way they'd always seemed to fix things. If money was tight or jobs were lost, they still always seemed to manage. And they'd stayed together. Not because they had to, but because they loved each other. Emily found it so hard to live up to that kind of example.

However, she could say none of this to Luke. What would he think of her if he knew? The last thing she wanted was to lay out a list of her faults and failings.

"And what took you to Calgary?"

She simply lifted an eyebrow.

"Ah," he chuckled, understanding. "Sam's father?"

She nodded, finally taking a seat at the table and curling her hands around the mug. The sun was up over the knoll now and gleaming brightly in the kitchen. This was where the questions would end. She had no desire to tell Luke the sordid details of the split. There would be no more breakfasts for two. She was here to work. It was glorious just to be able to make her own decisions now. She just kept telling herself that. Her parents didn't know she'd had to give up her house or that she hadn't received any child support. She'd been too proud to tell them. She'd been certain she'd turn things around before they got to this point. And she would. She just needed a little more time and a solid plan.

"And you?" To keep him from prying further into her personal life, she turned the tables. "You've been here your whole life, I suppose."

"Of course."

"The girls didn't care to be farmers?"

He looked at her over the rim of his mug, his blue gaze measuring. Luke Evans was no pushover, Emily realized. He saw right through her intentions. It should have put her off, but it didn't. Everything about Luke was intelligent, decisive. It was crazily sexy.

"The 'girls', as you say, got married and started their own families. Joe manages a farm-equipment dealership—he's the proud daddy this morning. Liz's husband is a schoolteacher. They both know their way around a barn, but that's not their life now."

"So you handle this alone?" She put the mug down on the table.

"I have some hired help." His lips made a thin line and his gaze slid from hers. Subject closed.

But she pressed on. "Then what about the Evans and Son on the sign? What about your dad and mom? How long have they been gone?"

He pushed out his chair and put his mug on top of his plate, taking the stack to the cupboard next to the sink. "I've got to get going. I have to get the boys started on their own this morning so I can run into town."

Emily knew she had gone too far. Something about his parents pushed a button. She had sensed it when she'd seen their picture, when he'd looked into their empty bedroom and again just now when she'd asked about them.

"About town...you really are short of groceries. Could we

go with you? We won't take extra time. We can shop while you run your errands."

He reached for his hat and plunked it on his head. To Emily, it seemed like armor to hide behind. And it added inches to his height.

Maybe some people didn't appreciate a closet full of fresh-smelling clothes, shining floors and a good meal, but she'd bet Luke would. She'd bet anything that he'd grown up exactly that way. His sisters had moved on, apparently to fulfilling, happy lives. Why hadn't Luke? Not that the farm wasn't successful. But it felt like a piece of the puzzle was missing.

"I can't expect you to cook without food, I suppose," he replied. "Be ready about nine, then. I need to get back as soon as I can."

"Yes, boss," she replied, putting his dishes in the sink to wash up.

It was all back to the status quo until he reached the screen door and then she heard his voice call quietly.

"Emily?"

She went to the doorway. "Yes?"

He smiled. "Good pancakes."

The screen door shut behind him, but Emily stared at it a good ten seconds before making her feet move.

Yes, indeed. She could wow Luke Evans in the kitchen. And she knew exactly what would be on the menu tonight.

CHAPTER FOUR

LUKE GAVE THE ratchet another turn and adjusted the trouble light. When had it gotten so dark? He stood back, staring at the rusted parts that made up the baler. It needed love. It needed replacing. But this repair would hold him through this season. And if things went well, he'd talk Joe into a discount and buy a new one next year.

He made a few final adjustments and straightened, rubbing the small of his back. Between the trip to town, Cait and the baler, he'd spent all of half an hour in the fields today. He frowned. It wasn't how he liked to run things. He wasn't a boss who gave orders and disappeared. Here everyone worked together and shared the load. But what could he do? He'd left the repairs until after dinner as it was, working in the dim light.

"Hi."

He spun at the sound of the small voice and saw Sam standing before him in his bare feet and a pair of cotton pajamas. The boy was cute as a bug's ear, Luke acknowledged, with his brown curls and wide chocolate eyes like his mother's. Eyes that seemed to see everything. Luke wiped his hands on a rag and tucked the end into his back pocket. "Shouldn't you be up at the house? In bed?"

A light blush darkened Sam's cheeks as his gaze skittered away for a moment. "I couldn't sleep. It's too hot."

"Your mom would open the window."

"She said she didn't want to hear a peep out of me," Sam admitted, and Luke hid a smile. Not hear a peep, so sneaking out of the house was okay?

"Then you'd better hightail it back in there, don't you think? You don't want your mom to be mad."

Sam swallowed and nodded and turned away, only to turn back again. "Why don't you like my mama?"

Luke's hands dropped to his sides as Sam asked the point-blank question. "What makes you think I don't like her?" he asked.

"Because you never said anything to her at supper. And she made veal. I helped. She only does that when it's special."

The veal had been good, as had the pasta and salad. Certainly much fancier than he was used to making for himself. "I suppose I had my head full of everything I need to do. I don't usually have company at the dinner table. I guess I'm not one for conversation."

Why on earth was he explaining this to a five-year-old boy? Besides, he knew it was a feeble excuse. He hadn't known what to say to her. He'd walked in to a house smelling of furniture polish and the fragrant lilacs she'd cut and put in one of his mother's vases she'd unearthed from somewhere. He'd instantly been transported to a time when the house had been filled with family. His mother's warm smiles. His dad's teasing. All of it had been taken from him in what felt like an instant, and he knew the chances of history repeating itself were too good to fool around with. But today he'd been taken back to a happier time.

He'd looked at Emily and felt the noose tightening. All through the meal he thought of her as she'd looked that morning as they ate alone in the quiet kitchen, with her pretty smiles and soft voice. It had felt domestic. Alarm bells had gone off like crazy in his head. He knew the signs. Watchfulness.

Blushes. He was as guilty of it as she was, and he had kept his distance ever since very deliberately. He'd had no idea what to say to her.

"I think you hurt her feelings," Sam persisted. His tone turned defensive and his brown eyes snapped. "My mama's a nice lady," he announced, lifting his chin as if daring Luke to dispute it, an action so like his mother Luke found it hard not to smile. "She cooks good and reads me stories and does all the best voices with my dinosaur puppets."

This was Luke's problem. He was too soft. He already felt sorry for the pair of them, and he didn't even really know the extent of their situation. Nor did he want to. He knew he shouldn't get involved. They were not his responsibility, and he didn't want them to be. He'd had enough responsibility to last a lifetime, and even though his sisters were on their own there was still the issue of his father's ongoing care. Emily was the housekeeper. Full stop.

Even Cait, in the first bloom of motherhood, had sensed something was up today. He'd said nothing, not wanting to mention Emily or her kid, instead dutifully admiring baby Janna. His sister was happy, but a family was not for him. So why did seeing her with Joe and her baby make him feel so empty? It was like that every time he saw Liz's girls, too. They thought he didn't particularly care for children. But the sorry truth was he knew he would never have any of his own and keeping his distance was just easier.

"I like your mom just fine, and you're right, supper was good. But my job is to fix this baler so we can roll up the hay out there and have feed for the winter."

Sam scowled. "Mama told me if we didn't stay here we had to go to Grandma and Grampa's. I don't even know what they look like."

Luke leaned against the bumper, watching Sam with keen eyes. When had she said such a thing? Before arriving or after he'd given her the job? He found the answer mattered to him. And how could Sam not know his grandparents? Regina wasn't so far from Calgary as to prevent visits.

"Oh, you must remember them."

But Sam shook his head. "My mama says they would be excited to see me because they haven't since I was a baby."

Three years. Maybe four, if what he said was true. Luke frowned. Even though he'd only known her a few days, he pictured Emily as the type to be surrounded by family. What had kept them apart?

"You should go on up to the house," he said, more firmly this time. "You don't want to get in trouble with your mom, Sam. Go on now."

Sam's lips twisted a little. "You don't like me either," he announced.

"What does it matter if I like you or not?" Luke was feeling annoyed now, having his character called out by a boy. Besides, it wasn't a matter of liking or not. It went so much deeper. Self-preservation, if it came to that. There was too much at stake for him to get all gushy over babies and such. "You get on up to bed."

Sam's little lip quivered but his eyes blazed. "That's all right. My dad doesn't like me either and my mama and I do just fine."

He spun on his toes and ran back to the house.

Luke sighed, watching him depart. He'd been sharp when he hadn't meant to be. It wasn't Sam's fault—or Emily's for that matter—that the years of stress and responsibility had worn him down. The boy had been through enough with his parents splitting up—Emily had as much as said so last night. He felt a moment of guilt, knowing Sam was feeling the loss of his father keenly. Did Sam never see him, then?

He rubbed a hand over his face, blew out a breath. Emily's domestic situation was none of his concern. Why he continually had to remind himself of that was a bit of a mystery. He turned out the trouble light and felt for a moment the satisfaction of another day done.

Followed by the heavy realization of all that remained to do tomorrow. And the day after that.

He squared his shoulders. "Suck it up, Evans," he mumbled to himself, shaking his head. Darn the two of them anyway. They'd had him thinking more over the last two days than he had in months, and not just about himself. About her, and the series of events that had landed her on his doorstep just at the moment he needed her most.

Emily was wiping up the last of the dishes and Sam was already sound asleep in bed when Luke returned to the house in the twilight. Sam had worked alongside her most of the afternoon, helping her dust the rooms and fetching things as she needed them. The bathroom fixtures shone and the floors gleamed again, and she sighed, not only from exhaustion but also from satisfaction. Sam had sometimes been more of a hindrance than a help, but it had been worth it to see the smile on his face and the pride he took in helping. It hadn't been until he'd nearly nodded off over his dinner that she'd realized he'd missed his afternoon nap.

Now he was tucked away in the small room, his dark head peaceful on the pillow. Meanwhile Emily had dishes to finish and the last of the dry sheets to put back on the spare beds before she could call it a night.

She heard Luke come in through the screen door and her heart did a little leap. It seemed so personal, having the run of his house, making herself at home. She heard the thump of his boots as he put them on the mat by the door and pictured him behind her. Now her pulse picked up as she heard his stockinged feet come closer. To her surprise he picked up the frying pan and moved to put it in the cupboard.

"Mr. Evans...you don't have to do that." She avoided his eyes as she picked up the last plate to dry.

"It's no biggie. I'm done for the day and you're not."

His shoulder was next to hers as he reached for another pot, the close contact setting off the same sparks as she'd felt at dinner. His jeans had been dirty with a smear of grease on one thigh, and his T-shirt had borne marks of his afternoon of work, but he'd gone into the downstairs bath and come to the table with clean hands and face and a few droplets of water clinging to his short hair.

It had been the wet hair that had done it. The tips were dark and glistening, and paired with the stubble on his chin it was unbelievably attractive. The economical way that he moved and how he said exactly what he meant, without any wasted words. He'd spoken to Sam only briefly during dinner, making little conversation before heading outside again. He hadn't even commented on the food, even though she'd pulled out all the stops and fussed with her favorite veal-and-pasta recipe. Emily tried not to be offended. Perhaps it was just his way. Perhaps he'd lived alone so long he wasn't used to making mealtime conversation. And that was quite sad when she thought about it.

"But our agreement..."

He put his hand on her arm and she stilled, plate in hand. She couldn't look at him. If she did, the color would seep into her cheeks. He was touching her. *Touching her,* and her skin seemed to shiver with pleasure beneath his fingers.

"Please," she said quietly. "This is my job. Let me do it."

"Pride, Emily?"

He used her first name and the sound of it, coming from his lips in the privacy of the kitchen, caused her cheeks to heat anyway. His hand slid off her arm and she realized she was holding the plate and doing nothing with it. She made a show of wiping the cloth over its surface. "Just stating the obvious."

"Who do you suppose cleans up when I'm here alone? I didn't realize putting a few things away would be a problem."

Oh, lordy. What right did she have to be territorial? "That's not what I meant," she replied hastily, putting the plate on the counter and reaching into the sink to pick up the last handful of cutlery. "Of course it's your kitchen..."

"Emily."

"You have more right to it than I do..."

She was babbling now, growing more nervous by the second as she felt his steady gaze on her. She bit down on her lip. She wouldn't say any more and make a bigger fool of herself. What did it matter if he put a dish away? She was the one caught up in a knot, determined to do everything perfectly. And why? She already knew that trying to be perfect didn't mean squat when it came down to it. She let out a slow breath, trying to relax.

"Why won't you look at me?"

She did then. She looked up into his eyes and saw that the blue irises were worried, making it impossible to maintain the distance she desired.

"You're paying me to do a job, so I should be the one to do it. If that's pride, then so be it."

"You're a stubborn woman, aren't you?"

Her lips dropped open and then she clamped them shut again, trying to think of a good reply. "I prefer determined."

"I just bet you do."

"Did you get the baler fixed?" She was desperate to change the subject, to turn the focus off herself and her failings. "I expect you'll be glad to be back in the fields tomorrow," she carried on, sorting the last of the cutlery into the drawer. The thought of the fields and waving alfalfa made her smile, gave her a sense of well-being. It had to be the peace and quiet, that was all. It had nothing to do with Luke Evans, or picturing him on top of a gigantic tractor in a dusty hat and even dustier boots.

"I can't expect the boys to handle things alone. I'll be glad to be back out with them again. I may be late for dinner to-morrow. Just so you know."

Oh, goodness, they were back to that again. She brushed her hands on her pants and inhaled, trying to appear poised. How could she explain that she'd actually enjoyed cleaning the homey farmhouse? That she'd felt more at home cooking a simple meal than she'd felt in a long time? Cooking anything elaborate for her and Sam seemed pointless, and she'd missed it.

"Thank you for letting me know. I'll plan something that keeps well, then. If you don't mind Sam and I going ahead."

"Of course not. Emily…" he paused and she gave in to temptation and looked up at him. He could look so serious, but something about his somber expression spoke to her. There was more to Luke than was on the surface. She was sure of it.

Their gazes clung for several seconds before he cleared his throat. "What I mean to say is, it is just great to have supper on the table when I come in and something better than a sandwich. It's a real nice thing to look forward to."

It was as heartfelt a comment as she'd guess Luke could come up with, and she took it to heart. She couldn't find the words to tell him that though, so she simply said, "Sam doesn't have such discerning taste. It was nice to have a reason to put together a real meal."

His gaze plumbed hers. "There was a reason I advertised for a housekeeper. The place looks great. And dinner was really good, Emily. I probably should have said so before."

She'd been slightly put out that he'd barely acknowledged

her efforts earlier, but the compliment still did its work, even though it was delayed. "I'm glad you liked it."

Why was he being nice to her now? She should be glad, relieved about all of it. But it threw her off balance. She furrowed her brow. Either she wanted his compliments and approval or she didn't. She wished she could make up her mind which.

"You're a very good cook."

"It was…"

She paused. So what if it was what she'd used to make for special occasions? She was tired of giving Rob any power. He had no business here. He had no business in her life anymore. He'd forfeited that privilege, and she'd done her share of crying about it. The only person keeping him front and center was her. "It is one of my favorites."

"So what's the story of Emily Northcott?" Luke folded up the dish towel and hung it over the door of the stove. "I mean, you must have a place in Calgary. Sam's father must be helping. Why pick a position that takes you away from home?"

Of course he'd ask right at the moment she'd decided not to mention Rob again. But the question struck a nerve. Somehow she wanted him to know. She wanted him to realize that she had tried everything she could to make things right. She already thought of him as stubborn rancher, a bit of a strong, silent type but she'd glimpsed moments of compassion, too. How would he remember her after she moved on? Not as a victim. Never that. She wanted him to see what she wanted to see in herself. Strength. Resourcefulness. Pride, but not vanity.

"I was a stay-at-home mom. Once I got pregnant and my ex started working, we agreed on a plan. I had my degree in science, and I put Rob through school by working for a laboratory. The idea was for him to start work and then he'd support me as I took my pharmacy degree. But then we had

Sam, and Rob said he would support us both. I was thrilled. Having Sam changed everything. Being his mom was the best job I'd ever had. I know it's not a job in the strict sense, but I really felt like I was doing something important, making a home for us, bringing him up. And I was thankful to have that choice. I know not everyone does."

Remembering those days stung. Rob had pretended the arrangement was perfect, but in the end it wasn't what he'd wanted. Emily had been too blind to see it until it was too late. "And then he left."

She cast a furtive look at the stairway, knowing Sam was asleep but still worried that if he woke up he'd hear her talking.

Luke followed her gaze. "You don't want him to hear us talking about it?"

Emily nodded, relieved he'd taken the hint so quickly. "He's been through enough. He's asleep, but any mention of his dad and he gets so upset."

"He thinks his dad doesn't like him."

Her head snapped around. "What?"

"He told me. He said I don't like him and his dad doesn't like him and that he does just fine." He pinned her with a steady look. "He's quite a kid, actually. But it made me wonder. Are you fine, Emily?"

She ignored the question, instead focusing on thoughts of Sam. Did he really believe that? That his father didn't like him? Sadness warred with anger at the situation. She hated that he didn't feel loved by both parents.

"I'm sorry he said that to you," she whispered, faltering for a moment, letting the despair in for just a second. Then she closed it away. There was nothing productive in feeling sorry for herself. "I'll have him apologize, Luke."

His gaze darkened and his jaw tightened. "No need. He

was just being honest. He's a good kid. You've done a good job with him. It's not easy being a single parent."

The compliment went to her heart. "Thank you. But I worry about what he's missing. If I'm enough, you know?"

"You just do the best you can."

She leaned back against the counter, looked up at Luke, wondering at the tight tone of his voice. What did he know of it? And yet she got the feeling he somehow understood. "I can't even put food on the table at the moment," she admitted.

His face flattened with alarm. "It's that bad?"

"Let's go outside," she suggested. Luke was standing too close again and she needed the fresh air and open space.

They left the porch light off to keep the Junebugs away, and Emily sat on the step, letting the first stars provide the light while they waited for last dregs of twilight to fade and the moon to rise. She had been at the ranch for two days, and the whole time Luke had felt like a boss, or like a complete stranger. But not tonight. Tonight he felt like an ally, despite the fact that they barely knew one another. It had been a long time since she'd had an ally. Since she'd had an unbiased ear to talk to.

Emily breathed in the fresh prairie air and the heavy scent of lilacs. "I love these," she said quietly. "Nothing smells better than lilacs."

Luke sat down beside her and the air warmed.

"My mother planted them," he said, putting his elbows on his knees and folding his hands. "I'm not much for flower gardens, I don't have time. But I've always tried to keep her lilacs. They smelled nice on the table tonight. Mom used to do that, too."

"What happened to her?"

"She died when I was nineteen. Brain aneurism."

Emily heard the grief in his voice even though it had to be ten years or more since her death. "I'm sorry, Luke."

He coughed. "It's all right. Right now we're talking about you. And why your ex was crazy enough to leave you and Sam and not even provide for both of you."

His words reached inside and illuminated a place that had been dark for a very long time.

"When he left, I had to start looking for work. No one wanted someone who hadn't been in the workplace for five years. Technology has changed. I had no references—the staff where I'd worked was all new. Rob hasn't paid a dime in child support." She twisted her fingers together as she looked over at Luke. "Not one."

"Surely a judge…"

Emily laughed bitterly. "Oh, yes. But it was an Alberta court and Rob moved to British Columbia. And I don't have the funds to fight him on it."

"I'm sorry. Of course you've had a difficult time of it."

She hadn't anticipated a helping hand and a caring tone. Not from a stranger. In a few stolen moments, Luke Evans had shown her more consideration than she'd had from any other quarter in several months. Then she reminded herself that she had promised to rely only on herself and she straightened her shoulders.

"It could have been worse," she admitted. "He didn't hurt us. Not physically. He just left. Said our life wasn't what he wanted and he was starting over."

"It doesn't always take punches to leave scars."

And, oh, she knew he was right. "Rob did lots of damage. They're just the kinds of scars that you can't see. I think they take longer to heal, too. The money is a practical difficulty, but the real kicker is how he has washed his hands of Sam. Sam is his son. I don't understand how a dad does that, Luke. I don't understand how I could have been so wrong. His abandonment made me question every single thing I thought I'd known about myself."

Luke was silent for a few moments. Then he said quietly, "You can't blame yourself for everything."

Emily wanted him to see she wasn't the kind of woman who let life happen to her. She was resourceful. But the kind way he was treating her was throwing her off balance. She'd wanted to create distance between them and instead she felt that he understood, perhaps even better than her friends in Calgary had. How was that possible?

The Junebugs thumped against the screen door, trying to get inside to the light that shone from the kitchen. Luke got up and brushed a hand down his jeans. "Let's walk," he suggested.

They strolled down the lane towards the road, past the mowed grass and to a cedar fence that was ornamental rather than functional. At the bottom Luke turned to her and she swallowed, feeling out of her league being alone with him like this. Unlike the fence, his appearance was for function rather than flash and just about the sexiest thing she'd ever seen, from the shorn hair to the faded jeans and dark T-shirt. The shirt clung in such a way that she could see the shape of his muscles, made strong by years of farm work. The sight of him with the moon behind him was something she knew she'd carry with her for a long time, burned on her mind as surely as the straightforward E of the Evans brand.

He was so completely opposite to the men she knew. It made her nervous and, at the same time, exhilarated. She told herself that after a year of being alone it was just a reaction. One that would go away as soon as she left the ranch.

"You didn't see it coming, did you?" Luke picked up the last thread of their conversation.

It hurt to talk about Rob. Not because she still loved him, but because she'd been so blind. While she wanted to blame him entirely, she couldn't help wondering if she might have done something differently. "He just announced one day that he was moving to start a new business. Said it was something he had to do for himself." She shook her head as though she still couldn't believe it. "I thought he meant he'd get started and we'd follow later. But he didn't. It wasn't just a job. He wanted his freedom and he took it."

She rubbed the toe of her sandal in the dusty dirt, making a swirly pattern that turned into a heart with a winding tail. "We had some savings that I protected once I realized what was going on. I needed to pay for housing, food. Clothing." She'd moved the savings money knowing that if Rob wanted to claim it, he'd end up creating more problems for himself. "We've been living on that while I tried to find a job to support us both."

Luke said a not-so-nice word that made Emily snort with surprised laughter.

"I called him that several times, too, over the last year. And I'll admit, I waited, thinking he'd come to his senses, that it was just a sort of crisis he'd get out of his system and we could put it all back together. But when he didn't, and the bills were piling up and the bank account dwindling, I filed for divorce and support."

"Sometimes life throws you one hell of a monkey wrench and all you can do is deal. Put one foot in front of the other," Luke replied.

Emily looked over at him, but his face was shadowed in the dark. Was that the voice of experience? His mother had passed away years ago. That must have been difficult. There was so much she didn't know about Luke Evans. On one hand she wanted to know more, to find some sort of solidarity with someone. On the other she knew she'd be better off to leave well enough alone, so she kept the questions on her tongue unsaid.

They turned and started walking back towards the house.

An owl called from a nearby line of trees and Emily jumped at the sound, chafing her arms with her hands.

"You're cold."

"No, it's good," she replied. "I needed this. I needed to get away. So did Sam. That's the real reason we left Calgary. Everything there was a reminder to Sam of our old life. He couldn't move past just wanting it back—how could he? He's not quite five. He doesn't understand. *I* don't understand. Sam just wanted Daddy to come home. He wanted family vacations and a huge pile of presents under the Christmas tree. I couldn't provide all of that on my own. Lord knows I did my best."

Emily shoved her hands into her pockets. "I'm not lazy, Luke. I applied for jobs for months. Anything I found was minimum wage or shift work or both. On minimum wage I can't afford babysitting. And shift work is horrible for finding good child care." She pursed her lips. "But this job is the best of both worlds. I get to do something I'm good at *and* be with my son. I've sold the Calgary house and I'm going to start over." She smiled, but it didn't chase away the cold. "I hope. I suppose if it doesn't work, there's always my parents. But no one wants to move back in with Mom and Dad, do they?"

Luke halted in the middle of the driveway. He looked up at the house, then up at the sky, and finally blew out a breath. She watched his Adam's apple bob as he swallowed. "It might not be so bad," he said quietly as the owl hooted. He turned to her and she felt her chest constrict beneath his gaze.

"But I don't think you'll need to worry. You strike me as the kind that always lands on her feet, Emily."

Luke studied her face as she smiled up at him. There was no denying that Emily was beautiful. But there was more. There was a quiet resolve to her that was equally attractive. She was a hard worker—he could tell that in the sheer volume of tasks she'd accomplished today. Even as her world spun out of control, she seemed in charge of it. Grounded. Calm in the middle of a storm. Sam thought the sun rose and set in her, because she put him first. He remembered the way she'd smoothed Sam's hair today, or had firmly made him mind his manners during dinner. Her kid was damned lucky.

"I hope you're not saying that just to be nice. I don't want pity, you know."

"Would I say anything for the sole purpose of being nice?" He raised an eyebrow.

"Good point." Her eyes sparkled up at him and he felt an unusual knot in his gut as her tongue wet her lips.

It was only a partial lie. He did feel sorry for her. Sorry that she'd been hurt and sorry she was having to deal with things alone. He knew all too well how that felt. To know that everything rests on your shoulders. To know that any decision you make affects others forever. He'd wished for a helping hand so many times when he was younger, first when his mom had died and then when his dad fell sick with Alzheimer's. He knew what it was to bear the weight of a family on his shoulders. In the past two days he'd questioned his sanity in letting Emily and Sam stay, but now that he knew a little more about their situation, he was glad.

And he was smart enough to know that if he told her such a thing she'd be furious. He was on good terms with their friend, Pride.

Meanwhile his body was tense just from being near her. He only wanted to help. Why then did just the soft scent of her, the sound of her voice, make his body tighten?

"If we keep on as we've started, I think we'll get along just fine," he said, thinking it sounded incredibly hokey, but he had to say something. She was a mother, for God's sake. A mother with a ton of baggage she was carrying around. The fleeting impulse to kiss her was beyond crazy. That was definitely a complication he didn't need.

"I think so, too," she agreed.

They drew nearer the house, the walk coming to an end and with it their confidences in the dark. "Thank you for telling me about your situation," he said. He looked up and thought he saw movement at the curtain of Sam's room, but in the dark he couldn't be sure. Was the boy watching them? Now that he knew more about it, he could understand Sam being mixed up and protective of his mother. Not that it excused bad behavior. There'd be no more sneaking out after bedtime.

"It was only fair. I'm a stranger, right? You agreed to this arrangement without knowing anything about me. You don't need me to bring trouble to your door. No fear of that, anyway," she said softly. "Rob doesn't care enough to come after us."

She tried to make it sound as though she didn't care, but he knew she did. He wondered what kind of man didn't love his kid enough to keep in touch, to know where they were? Luke didn't want the added responsibility of children, but if he had them, he'd do a damn sight better job of parenting than that.

He wasn't sure how a man could let his wife go either. Especially one like Emily.

"I'm sorry," he offered, and meant it.

"Me, too." She sighed in the moonlight. "One of these days you'll have to tell me your story," she suggested.

"Not likely," he replied quickly. "Not much to tell."

She laughed, and it seemed to lighten the evening. "Now why don't I believe that? You're pretty close-mouthed when it comes to your own saga." She grinned, looking impish in the moonlight. "But you have been kind and generous, letting us both stay."

"No one's ever accused me of being either," he replied, their steps slowing, scuffing along in the dirt of the driveway.

"Most would say I'm practical." He'd had to be, getting the girls the rest of the way to adulthood and making sure the farm could support them all. There hadn't been time for what most twenty-year-olds had been doing—working hard, but playing harder. It made him think of the old Bible verses from Sunday school, about leaving childish things behind.

"Do you ever wish you'd finished your degree, Emily?"

She looked up at him, putting one hand on the wood railing of the steps. "When the money was dwindling, I confess I did. But sometimes you exchange old dreams for new ones. After five years, this is what I do best. I love being home with Sam. I loved looking after my house and cooking and doing all the special things I couldn't do if I'd been working all day. I was very fortunate, you know?"

"And do you ever think of going back?"

She paused, her expression thoughtful. "Maybe. But not pharmacy. Something else. Something that uses my strengths. I guess I just don't know what that is yet."

For several seconds they stood there staring at each other. Luke's gaze dropped to her lips and then back up to her eyes. Maybe it was the moonlight, or the way her hair curled around her collar, or the soft sound of her voice that reached inside of him and made him want. And what he wanted was to kiss her—for the second time in ten minutes.

Which was absolutely plumb crazy. There were a dozen solid reasons why he shouldn't.

And he wouldn't.

But he couldn't help thinking about it just the same.

"Well, Mr. Evans, I believe we both have early starts in the morning." She turned to go up the steps. "There is a lot more to be done around here. I think tomorrow I'll examine your vegetable garden."

Lord, she had a lot of pride. But Luke understood that. It made him want to lend his assistance. "I haven't tended to the weeds in a while. The potatoes are sure to need hoeing."

He took a step forward, and his gaze dropped to her full, lush lips. He was standing in the moonlight with a beautiful woman and all he could do was talk about gardens and chores. Had it been that long since he'd dated that he had lost all concept of conversation? The moment stretched out and he leaned forward, just a bit until the floral scent he now recognized as hers filled his nostrils.

He reached out and took her fingers in his hand and felt them tremble.

This was ridiculous. She'd just got through telling him about her disintegrated marriage and he was contemplating coming on to her? He straightened, took a step back.

"It's been a long day," she whispered, pulling her fingers away and tucking them into her pockets. He heard the nervous quaver in her voice and knew she understood exactly what direction his thoughts had taken.

"I'll see you in the morning."

She went inside, closing the door quietly behind her, but for several minutes Luke sat on the porch, thinking.

How could a man just walk out on his family that way? Leave his responsibilities behind? A real man did what needed to be done. His dad had instilled that in him from the time he was younger than Sam. But just because Northcott had left his wife and kid didn't mean they were suddenly Luke's responsibility. For the last decade, he'd had the ranch to worry about, and his sisters until they'd made their way on their own. Now it was the ranch and his father's failing health. It was more than enough. He didn't need to take on any wounded strays.

He just had to remember to shut down any more thoughts

of kissing her. Uncomplicated. That was exactly how this was going to stay. And after she was gone, he'd manage on his own once more.

Just like he always did.

CHAPTER FIVE

EMILY CALLED HER parents first thing after breakfast, once Luke was out of the house and she'd sent Sam upstairs to get dressed. She kept the call brief, merely letting them know of the change of situation and a number where they could contact her.

Then she hung up, feeling like a big fat coward. Her parents had no idea how tight things had become financially, and she didn't want them to either. She knew her dad would insist on helping, something they could not afford now that he was retired. Maybe Luke was right. Maybe she did have too much pride. But there was satisfaction in knowing she was doing it herself. And refusing help also meant she was one-hundred-percent free to make her own choices. She liked that.

She liked being at the Evans ranch, too. She had a purpose, something that had seemed to be missing for too long. She hung out a load of laundry, smelling the lilacs on the air as she pinned the clothes on the line. Sam handed her the clothespins, his dark hair shining in the morning sunlight. "I like it here," she said easily, taking another of Luke's T-shirts and hanging it by the hem. "What about you, Sam?"

Sam shrugged. "It's quiet. And I haven't been able to see much."

"Maybe this afternoon we can take a walk. Search out some wildflowers and birds' nests." Emily felt a catch in her heart, wishing for a moment that he had a brother or sister to keep him company. "I can ask around about some day camps, too, if you like."

"I like the horses," Sam replied, handing her another clothespin. "Do you think I'll be able to ride one?"

Emily frowned. Sam was five and a full-grown horse was so...huge. "I don't know," she answered honestly. "Luke has quarter horses, and he's very busy."

Sam looked disappointed. "Don't worry," she added, ruffling his hair. "Once we get settled it'll all come around all right. Promise."

Sam went off to color in an activity book while Emily fussed around the kitchen, taking a tray of chicken breasts out to thaw for supper. Their conversation had made her think. Keeping Sam busy might be harder than she'd thought. She'd have to think of ways to keep him entertained. She looked at the chicken and then around at the kitchen. Luke had thanked her for the meal last night but it was clear to her that he appreciated plain cooking. Why not keep Sam occupied today by baking? He loved helping her at home. An apple cake, perhaps. And cookies. Sam loved rolling cookies.

With the house tidied and the laundry under control, Emily liked the thought of spending the day in the kitchen, mixing ingredients. She hummed a little as she got out a mixing bowl and began setting out what she'd need. She imagined Luke coming in to rich spicy smells and the smile that would turn his lips up just a bit at the edges.

Her hand stilled on a bag of sugar. Why should it matter if he smiled at her or not? Her stomach did a flutter as she remembered the way his hands had squeezed her fingers last night. He was being nice, that was all. Maybe that was it. He didn't come across as a typically nice person, so last night's chat in the dark had thrown her off balance.

She knew the recipes by heart and when Sam came back

downstairs, they began mixing, rolling and baking. The apple cake, with its topping of brown sugar and cinnamon was cooling on the stovetop and Sam took a fork and pressed on the peanut butter cookies in a crisscross pattern. She'd just sat Sam up to the table with a few warm cookies and a glass of milk when the screen door slammed. Emily pressed a hand to her belly, brushing the flour off the white-and-blue apron she'd found in a drawer. Luke was back already? And the kitchen was still a mess, with dirty dishes and flour dusting the counter surfaces!

"Luke, you here?"

The voice was male but it definitely wasn't Luke's. Emily bit down on her lip as Sam paused mid-drink and looked at her.

"Wait here," she instructed Sam, and took a breath. Whoever was there was comfortable enough to come into the house without knocking.

"Hello?" She stepped through the swinging door of the kitchen and moved towards the foyer, where she could hear footsteps. "Can I help you?"

A tower of a man came around the corner. He topped Luke by a good three inches, and Luke had to be close to six feet. Instead of Luke's uniform of jeans and T-shirts, this man wore dress trousers and a shirt and tie, and he carried a box cradled under one arm. Short-cropped walnut-brown hair and warm brown eyes assessed her. "You must be the new housekeeper," he said, but he smiled, making the to-the-point introduction friendly rather than brusque. "I'm Joe. Luke's brother-in-law."

This was Cait's husband, Emily remembered. The one who worked at the equipment dealership. "The new dad," she replied, holding out her hand. "Congratulations. I'm Emily Northcott."

His dark eyes were warm and friendly as he took her hand.

"My wife is very glad you're here at last. She was worried about her big brother managing everything." He inclined his chin for a moment. "It smells good in here."

She withdrew her hand from his, feeling unease center in her belly. When she'd met Luke and shaken his hand, there'd been a queer fluttering and the heat of his skin against hers. With Joe there was none of that. It shouldn't have been different. Luke wasn't any different. He was just a guy.

If that were true, why had she felt the curl of anticipation when the screen door had slammed?

Now his brother-in-law was here and she was feeling that she should play host. "There's coffee and warm cookies, if you'd like some," she invited.

"I wouldn't say no." He put the box on the floor by the door. "Cait in the hospital means cooking for myself right now. If you think Luke's bad in the kitchen…I think I can burn water. Cait got her mother's cooking skills, thank God."

Joe followed her into the kitchen and stopped at the sight of Sam at the table. "Your son?" he asked.

"Yes, this is Sam. Sam, this is Mr. Evans's brother-in-law, Joe."

"You're not a cowboy like Luke," Sam stated, taking the last half of his cookie and dunking it in his milk. Crumbs floated on the top of the creamy surface.

Joe looked down at himself and back up. "No, I guess you're right! I work at the tractor dealership in town."

"I could tell by your clothes."

Joe laughed while Emily resisted the compulsion to curb Sam's matter-of-fact observations.

"Believe it or not, Sam, I've done a fair share of farm jobs. Not like Luke, of course." Joe looked at Emily and winked. It was clear that Luke had already made a solid impression on her son. "But I've been known to lend a hand now and again."

"Luke has a four-wheeler and a tractor and horses. I haven't seen them yet, though. Not up close."

Sam's dark eyes were wide with honest disappointment. Emily hadn't realized that Sam had noticed all those things in addition to the horses. She wondered if she could convince Luke to take him for a ride on the quad or tractor one of these days.

She handed Joe a mug of coffee and put the cream and sugar in front of him as he sat at the table. "Is your wife coming home from the hospital soon?" She offered him a cookie.

"Maybe this afternoon."

"You must be excited."

His eyes gleamed. "We are. We've been waiting a long time for Janna to arrive. Cait has been worried about Luke, though. The ad for the housekeeper didn't get results and Cait is a mother hen. It's one less thing for her to worry about. And then I won't have to worry about *her.*"

It was clear to Emily by the way Joe spoke, from the gleam in his eyes, that he loved his wife very much. It was beautiful but caused a sad pang inside her. She'd thought she had that once. Had Rob ever looked at her that way? She'd thought so. Now she wondered if her radar had been flawed all along. She wasn't sure she could ever trust her judgment again.

"Look what the cat dragged in."

Luke stood in the doorway of the kitchen, his hat in his hands and a smile of pure pleasure on his face. "How's the new father?"

"Anxious to get my family home."

"Mom and baby?" Luke stepped inside the kitchen and Emily felt the disconcerting swoop again, the one that felt like riding the roller coaster at Calaway Park. Trouble.

"Home this afternoon, I hope. I brought your parts out that

you asked for. Have a cookie, Luke. They're mighty good. I get the feeling you lucked out with your housekeeper."

"I could have come in and picked them up." Luke angled Joe a telling look. "Unless Cait sent you out here to do a little recon."

Joe didn't even look away, just smiled crookedly at Luke. "I'm not in a position to say no to that woman at the moment," he replied. "And even if I tried, she'd remind me about the twelve hours of labor she just had to endure."

Luke took a cookie from the plate and met Emily's eyes across the kitchen. It was as if an electric wire sizzled between them, and she held her breath. Last night he'd come close to kissing her. At the time she'd put it down to her own fanciful thinking in the moonlight, but she was sure of it now. With his blue gaze flashing at her, she knew she'd been right.

He bit into the cookie and a few crumbs fluttered to the floor. She watched, fascinated, as his lips closed around the sweet and his tongue snuck out to lick away the bits that clung to his bottom lip.

Oh, dear.

She suddenly realized that Joe was watching them with one eyebrow raised and she forced a smile, grabbing a dishcloth and starting to run some water into the sink. "I'm afraid the kitchen is quite a mess," she said, knowing it was inane conversation but desperately needing to fill the gap of silence. "I'd better get started on these dishes."

"And I'd better get back to town." Joe stood up, brought his cup to the sink. "Nice to meet you, Emily."

"You, too. Congratulations again." She squeezed soap into the running water. She didn't dare look at him. She'd blush, she just knew it. She'd been horribly transparent when she'd met Luke's gaze.

"Thanks for bringing the parts out," Luke said, grabbing

another cookie. "I'm heading back out, but now I can get a start on them tonight."

A start? Emily's head swiveled around to look at him. Did he work from dawn until dusk every day?

"Oh, and I brought out some rhubarb," Joe added. "Liz sent it. She said if you couldn't use it now to freeze it. I'm betting Emily could work her magic on it though."

"I can try," she said softly, watching the two of them leave the kitchen and head to the front door.

It was all so normal. A family who cared and looked after each other. Even the idea that Joe had been sent to scope her out for the family didn't really bother her. It was what families did, she supposed. When Luke needed a tractor part, his brother-in-law brought it. Cait worried about him and his other sister sent rhubarb. It was their way of showing they cared. The kind of big family she'd always wanted and had never had.

Sam hopped down from his chair and asked if he could go play in the yard. She let him go, not wanting him to see the telltale moisture gathering in her eyes. She was a good mother. She knew that. She loved Sam and had never regretted staying home with him. But who was there for her?

She scrubbed at the mixing bowl that had held the cake batter and sniffed. Suddenly she wished for an older sister or brother. Someone she might have called when her life was falling apart to reminisce with about childhood. Someone to share her hurt with—and someone to make her laugh again.

Someone like Luke, last night. He'd listened. He'd even made her laugh a little. But Luke was different. There was nothing brotherly about the way she reacted when she was near him. That frankly scared her to death.

"I thought I'd bring you the rhubarb before I headed out."

For once she hadn't heard him come back in and his deep

voice shimmered along all her nerve endings. She swallowed, hating that he'd caught her in a moment of self-pity. "Thank you, Luke. I'll make sure I do something with it right away."

"Em?"

He shortened her name and the intimate feeling of being alone with him multiplied.

"Are you okay?"

She gave a little laugh. "Oh, it's foolishness. You caught me being a little sorry for myself, that's all."

"Why?"

He took a step closer.

She could hardly breathe. "I don't know your family, but I get the sense that you all look after each other. It's nice, that's all. I don't have any brothers or sisters."

"You've handled your situation all alone, haven't you?"

"Pretty much. Friends can only take so much of hearing your troubles, you know? I'm not very much fun these days. So many of them are couples, and I was suddenly the odd man out. They were Rob's friends, too, and it is awkward if you're suddenly picking sides. It was just…"

"Easier to stay away?"

She looked up, surprised yet again that he seemed to understand so easily. "Yes, I guess so. Sometimes I miss the easygoing, fun Emily I used to be."

"Taking the responsibility of the world on your shoulders tends to have that effect," he replied, coming to her and putting his wide hands on her arms. "You are doing the best you can, right?"

She swallowed, tried to ignore the heat from his hands soaking through the cotton of her shirt. "Taking care of Sam is everything to me." She blinked, feeling herself unravel at the kind way he was looking at her. "Not being able to support us makes me feel like such a failure."

He lifted one hand and gently traced his thumb beneath her eye, lifting the moisture away from the skin. "You are not a failure, Emily. You only fail if you stop trying. And I might not know you well, but I can see you're no quitter."

It was a lifeline to cling to and she shuddered in a breath. But when she looked up into his eyes, everything seemed to drop out of her, making her feel weightless, feel that the clock on the wall had suddenly stopped ticking.

His fingers tightened on her shoulder as he drew her closer. For a few precious seconds his lips hovered only an inch from hers. Her heart hammered, wanting desperately for him to kiss her and terrified that he actually might.

Then his breath came out in a rush and he moved back, wiping a hand over his face. "What am I doing?" he asked, more to himself than to her, she realized. Her face flamed with embarrassment. He'd stepped back, but she would have kissed him. If he'd stayed there a moment longer, she would have leaned in and touched his lips with her own.

"I'm sorry." He put his hands in his pockets and the blue heat she'd seen in his eyes was cool and controlled now. "That isn't why you're here. I overstepped, Emily. It won't happen again."

Why on earth was she feeling such profound disappointment? Kissing him would complicate everything! And there was Sam to consider. What if he saw them? He still hadn't quite grasped the unalterable fact that his father wasn't coming back.

"It would be confusing to Sam if he were to see," she said quietly. "And I am not in the market for a relationship. You must know that."

"I do. Of course I do." He had the grace to look chastened. "I don't play games, Emily. I'm not interested in romance either, and I won't toy with you. What happened just now was…an aberration."

He paused, and Emily knew he was measuring his words. What was he protecting? Luke seemed fine when he was dealing with others, but when it came to himself he was irritatingly closed off. He had been open and laughing with Joe, but with her he put the walls back up. She wondered why.

"I don't understand you at all, Luke. You can be very distant, and then last night it was almost as if you were right there in my shoes. Why is that?"

He stared out the window and she wondered if he was avoiding looking at her on purpose.

"I know what it's like to have so much responsibility on your shoulders, that's all. I was only twenty when I took over this farm, and I'm the oldest. Cait and Liz were still in their teens. It's not easy being thrust into the role of primary caregiver and provider. I understand that, Emily. After last night... let's just say I want to help you get your feet beneath you again."

Emily felt her pride take a hit. Had she really seemed that desperate? "Rescuing women and puppies, is that it?"

He frowned. "It's not like that. There was no rescuing involved. I did need help. It was such a relief to come inside last night and know that the house wasn't in shambles. To have a meal hot and waiting rather than throwing something together at the last minute. Why is it so hard for you to accept that this is important? I'm not a particularly charitable man, Emily. I'm not one for pretty words."

She pondered it for a moment, not liking the answer that came to her mind.

"Don't you think what you've done has value?"

He did know how to get in a direct shot, didn't he? Emily dropped her eyes and reached for a dish towel.

"Economics, Emily. The value of something goes up when it's in short supply. Believe me, I've had to keep up with the ranch and the house and...everything else on my own. I appreciate what you've done more than you know."

She wondered what he'd really been going to say in the pause. What everything? "You're just saying that."

"Why would I?"

He came close again. Emily could feel him next to her shoulder and wanted so badly to turn into his arms. She clenched her jaw. How needy could she be, anyway? So desperate that she'd let herself be swayed by a husky voice and a pair of extraordinary blue eyes? She'd gone months without so much as a hug. Wanting to lose herself in his embrace made her weak, and she couldn't give in. Her control was barely hanging on by a thread. She was afraid of what might happen if she let herself go. At the very least, she'd make a fool of herself, especially after their protests that neither of them were interested in romance. She didn't want to look like a fool ever again.

"Did *he* tell you it wasn't important?"

Emily didn't have to ask who *he* was. She'd told Luke enough last night for him to paint a fairly accurate picture. "Staying home with Sam was a mutual decision," she whispered. "But it didn't stop him from getting in the little digs that the financial burden of the family rested on his shoulders. And he never quite saw that while I didn't carry the finances, I looked after everything else, and gladly." She swallowed. "We decided together. I did have to remind him of that on occasion."

She twisted her hands in the dish towel, knowing if she turned her head the slightest bit she'd be staring into his eyes again. The temptation was there. To see if the flare in his eyes was real. Rob hadn't appreciated her. She knew that now. He'd shouldered the financial responsibility of their family and then he'd had enough. She didn't realize how much she needed the validation until she heard it from Luke's lips—a relative stranger who seemed to appreciate her more in two short days than anyone had in years.

"There are some things you can't put a price tag on," Luke said. "He was a fool."

Emily's pulse leapt. Yes, he had been a fool. She had put everything into their family only to be discarded. She turned to Luke then, dropping the dish towel to the countertop. It was a seductive thing, to feel that she was being seen. Really seen.

"I know," she whispered. "I know it in my head. It's harder to convince my heart."

A muscle ticked in Luke's jaw as silence dropped. Emily couldn't have dragged her gaze away if she'd tried. Their gazes meshed, pulling them together even as they both held back.

"Dammit," Luke uttered, then curled his hand around the nape of her neck and moved in to kiss her.

She was vaguely aware of lifting her hands and placing them on his arms. The skin below the hem of his T-shirt sleeve was warm, covering solid muscle from his long days of manual labor. Every square inch of Luke Evans was solid, a formidable, unbreachable wall. Except his mouth. Oh, his mouth. It was incredibly mobile, slanted over hers and making her weak in the knees. He tasted like peanut butter cookies and coffee and the way he was kissing her made her feel like a strawberry, sweet and ripening on the vine in the summer sun.

His muscles relaxed against hers, but with the easing off came a new and wonderful complication: he settled into the kiss now, pulling her body flush against his, making her feel that it could go on forever and nearly wishing it would. She melted into him, resting against the solid wall of his chest, surrendering.

His cell phone rang, the holster vibrating against her hipbone. The ring tone sounded abnormally loud in the quiet kitchen and Emily staggered backwards, holding on to the counter for support. For one sublime second Luke's gaze collided with hers, hot and perhaps a little confused. Blindly he reached for the phone and then the moment disintegrated into dust as he turned his attention to the display.

Emily grabbed at the discarded dish towel and began drying dishes, wiping each one with brisk efficiency before putting it on a clean portion of countertop. What had they done? Got completely carried away, that's what, and right after they'd said they wouldn't. Heat rushed to her cheeks and flooded through her body. It had been perfectly, wonderfully glorious.

But so wrong. If he'd set out to prove a point, he'd done it. She was vulnerable. Hungry for affection. She put down a mixing bowl and dropped her forehead to her palm. She'd been weak, when only minutes before she'd determined this wouldn't happen. How could she keep the promises she'd made to herself and to Sam if she indulged in such a lack of self-control?

"I've got to get going," Luke's voice came from behind her and she straightened, stiffening her spine.

"Of course. You have work to do."

"Emily..."

That one word—her name—seemed full of unasked questions. Was he feeling as uncertain as she was?

"Luke." She said it firmly, shutting down any doubts. This couldn't happen again. Thinking about whatever chemistry was zinging between them was bad enough. Acting on it was just wrong. She had a plan. It wasn't a perfect plan, but it would be good for her son. A mother did what she had to do. That included taking this job until she could find a more permanent situation.

"I...uh..."

Her throat constricted. She couldn't bear to hear him apologize or say what a mistake it had been.

"You'd better attend to whatever that was," she said, nodding at his phone.

"We'll talk later?"

One more complicated look and he spun on his heel, heading out the door again without waiting for her to answer.

Talk? Emily put her fingers to her lips. They were still humming from the contact with his. They wouldn't talk about this at all—not if she could help it.

CHAPTER SIX

LUKE MADE THE last turn around the field, leaving a swath of sweet-smelling grass behind him and a sense of relief in its wake. The sun shone benevolently down on him right now, but by tomorrow night that would change. The forecast was for rain and thunderstorms. As long as the fine weather held out for another day the first cut would be done and baled and, most importantly, dry. If everything went on schedule. And if the repairs he'd made to the baler held. A lot of ifs.

He checked his watch. Nearly lunch. The Orrick brothers had been raking the east field and would eat their meal in their truck. Luke could have brought his lunch with him, but he looked forward to going back to the house and seeing what Emily had cooked up. Usually he appreciated the thought of peace and quiet and solitude at mealtime. But lately he'd found himself looking forward to Emily's quiet greetings and Sam's chatter.

As he turned the tractor south towards home, he frowned. This wasn't something he should let himself get used to. Cooking or not, being around Emily wasn't the best idea. Not after yesterday. What had he been thinking, kissing her like that? He'd got carried away. She'd turned those liquid brown eyes on him, so hurt and insecure. She'd hate his pity, but he was sorry that she had to carry the weight of her family on her own, knowing there was no way out from beneath the weight of responsibility. Sorry that she'd been married to a man who didn't appreciate all she did. Her lip had quivered and he'd wanted to make it up to her somehow.

Oh, who was he fooling? He touched the throttle, speeding up as he hit the straight dirt lane. He had wanted to kiss her, plain and simple. Still did, if it came to that, even though he knew it was a huge mistake. He could justify it six ways from Sunday, but the truth was she was the prettiest thing he'd laid eyes on in forever. She was out here in the middle of nowhere, but she didn't turn up her nose like so many of the girls did these days—like ranching was some sort of second-class occupation. She breathed deeply of the air, enjoying the space and freedom. And the way she touched Sam, ruffling his hair and showering him with hugs. It was the sort of affectionate touch that was second nature to a mother. The kind he'd grown up with. His mother had been firm but loving. His father, too.

Until his mother had died and everything changed.

The house was in sight, and he spied Emily and Sam in the vegetable garden. For a moment it felt so incredibly right. But then the feeling grew heavy in his chest. It couldn't be *right*. Emily was far too hurt from her divorce, no matter what she said. And Luke liked Sam but he didn't want kids. He didn't want to be married, either. The last thing he wanted was the burden of caring for a family, risking putting them through what he'd been through. Each time he visited his father he was reminded of what the future could hold for him. Seeing his dad suffer quelled any ideas Luke had about a family of his own. No, he'd run the farm and leave the marriage and kids thing to his sisters.

And no matter what Emily said, she was the marrying kind. She wasn't the kind of woman a man trifled with. She certainly wasn't the type for an eyes-open-no-strings fling. So that left them right back at boss and employee.

He pulled up to the barn and wasn't surprised to see

Sam bounding along to greet him. He was a good kid. He minded his mother and was polite and didn't get into things he shouldn't get into. "Hey, Sam."

"Luke! We're weeding your garden and I only pulled up one bean." His face fell a little. "I hope that's okay."

"One little bean plant isn't going to make any difference, don't worry," Luke assured him. The boy had clearly forgiven him for any slights made earlier as he aimed a wide smile at Luke. He noticed Sam had lost his first tooth and couldn't help but smile back at the lopsided grin. "Tooth fairy give you anything for that?"

"A dollar," Sam announced proudly.

Luke cleared his head, pushing away the earlier thoughts of kissing Emily. Sitting on a tractor for hours always gave him way too much time to think. What was he so worried about? It wasn't like he was falling in love with her or anything. It had just been a kiss. Nothing to lose sleep over.

Except he had. It had been ten past midnight when he'd checked the alarm clock last night. Replaying the taste of her, the feel of her in his arms. He walked towards the garden with Sam, watching Emily bent over the tiny green plants. His gaze dropped to the curve of her bottom and his mouth went dry. She straightened, standing up in the row of peas and put her hands on her lower back, stretching.

Little pieces of her hair curled up around the edges of one of his baseball caps, the curved brim shading her eyes from the sun. She wore cutoff denim shorts and a T-shirt the same color as the lilacs by the front verandah, the cotton hugging her ribs, emphasizing her spare figure. His gaze caught on the long length of her leg and he swallowed. It was impossible to stop thinking about yesterday when he'd held her in his arms.

"We might actually get this first cut done before the weather changes," he remarked as he approached the rows of vegetables. Now he was reduced to talking about the weather? It wasn't a good sign when he felt the need to keep things to nice, safe topics. He looked over the garden. Half of it was neatly weeded and tended, the tiny shoots healthy and green. The other half was slightly scraggly. "Thank you for doing the garden. It was on my to-do list."

"It was no trouble. The inside of the house is under control now and it was too beautiful a day to waste. I like being outside, and so does Sam. Don't you Sam?"

Sam nodded, his bangs flopping. "Yup. Mom showed me what a pea plant looks like, and a bean and the carrots, too!" He held up a small pail. "And I took the weeds to the compost pile, too."

"You're a good help," Luke said, unable to resist the boy's excitement. How often had he done this very thing? All the kids had. Working in the garden had been part of their summer chores. "I like working in the outdoors, too."

"Mom said you're too busy to take me on the tractor or anything."

Luke angled his head and looked at Sam, assessing. Sam was what, almost five? At that age, Luke had already been helping in the barns and riding on the tractor with his dad. The memories were good ones, and Sam hadn't experienced anything like that.

"I'm going to be raking hay this afternoon. You can come with me if you like."

Maybe it was a bad idea. He was trying to keep his distance and he wasn't sure Emily would appreciate him encouraging her son. But neither could he stand the thought of the boy feeling alone, left out. Luke knew that helping his dad had made him feel a part of something. The sound of the machinery, the time out of doors, the sense of accomplishment. What could it hurt, just this once?

Sam's eyes lit up and he practically bounced on his toes. "Mom? Can I?"

Emily's dark eyes were centered on him again and he felt the same tightening as he had yesterday when he'd held her body against his. Lord, she'd been sweet and soft and when he'd kissed her every single thought in his brain had gone on vacation.

"You don't have to do that, Luke. You're busy. Sam can wait for another time."

Sam's shoulders slumped in disappointment and he scuffed a toe in the dirt, the action reminiscent of his mother. Clearly Sam had wanted to go, and it was no big deal having him on the tractor with him. Hadn't the boy suffered enough disappointments lately? Luke looked at Emily, knowing she was acutely unhappy with the path her life had taken. He knew she was trying to do her best, but that cloud of unhappiness affected Sam, too. She couldn't keep him tied to her apron strings forever.

"It's just a tractor ride," he answered. "I'm going to be sitting there anyway, raking what we cut yesterday. The boys will be coming along behind, doing the baling. No reason why he shouldn't come along. It'll be a chance for him to learn something new. And give you a little time to yourself."

"Please, Mom?"

She paused.

"He'll be safe with me, Emily. I promise. You have to let go some time."

Her gaze snapped to his and her lips thinned but he held his ground. Sam was a boy. He needed freedom to play and see and do things. Luke understood Emily being protective, but an afternoon in the sun would be good for him. Luke was not her ex. If he made a promise he'd keep it. "It's only a tractor ride," he repeated.

* * *

Emily paused, taken aback by Luke's words. Was she over-protective? She didn't think so. She was only focused on Sam feeling loved and secure. His expressive eyes had looked so hurt, so broken since his father left and she'd do anything to keep that from happening again. She didn't want Sam to get any hopes up.

But perhaps Luke was right. It was just a tractor ride, after all. Didn't Sam deserve some fun? "I'll think about it over lunch." She put off a firm decision, needing him to see that she wasn't going to accept being nudged or coerced. He should have done the courtesy of asking her in private. Heavens, he'd barely said two words to Sam the first few days and now here they were, seemingly thick as thieves.

"Lunch is ready, by the way. I made chicken salad this morning and a cobbler out of that rhubarb your sister sent."

He sent her a cheeky smile from beneath his hat. "You might have to stop treating me so well. I'll get round and fat." He stuck out his stomach and Sam giggled.

Emily pressed her lips together. The man was exasperating! It was almost as if he and Sam were in cahoots together. Which was probably preferable to his taciturn moodiness the first few days, but she didn't want Sam to get too attached. He could get a good case of hero worship without much trouble. And this job wasn't permanent.

Sam bounded on ahead to wash up and Emily took off her cap and shook out her hair. She looked straight ahead as she asked, "You might have asked me first, rather than putting me on the spot."

"What? Oh, I didn't think you'd mind. He did mention something about the tractor the other day, didn't he?"

"That's not the point."

His steps halted, churning up a puff of dust. "Look, I know you're worried about him and it's something he might find fun. I don't get your problem."

She angled him a look that said *Get real.* "My problem is, he's had too many promises made to him that have been broken. Have you seen how he looks at you? Like you hung the moon and the stars. He's been missing a father figure and suddenly here you are."

Luke laughed. "I doubt it. He snuck out of bed the other night and told me off for not complimenting you on your veal."

Emily's mouth dropped open. "He what?"

"Came to the shop and told me you were a nice lady and that his dad doesn't like him and he doesn't care whether I do either. Now, normally a five-year-old boy's opinion wouldn't bother me, but it occurred to me that perhaps I hadn't been as welcoming as I might have been. Don't read too much into it. Like I said, it's just a tractor ride."

Emily folded her hands together. "I guess I can't blame him for being protective. His trust has been shaken."

"Just his?" he asked quietly, walking along beside her again. "Are you really planning never to trust anyone again?"

How could he blame her for being a little gun-shy? "Let's just say trust is a valuable commodity and it has to be earned."

"Yes, and your ex is a prime example of earning it and then abusing it. There's more to building trust than time."

His words cut her deeply. She had trusted Rob and he'd ground her faith in him beneath his heel when he left. She'd made a lot of progress since then. She'd stopped blaming herself for everything. She'd stopped feeling so desperate. She'd started focusing on the good—as much as that was possible. But trust…that was something she wasn't sure she'd ever quite accomplish again.

"If you're so smart, what else is there?" She didn't bother to keep the annoyance out of her voice. Sometimes Luke was far too sure of himself. Like he had her all figured out.

"Actions. Hell, instincts, if it comes to that."

His observations made her uncomfortable, because her instincts had told her from the beginning that Luke was a man she could trust. And he'd kept his word about everything since her arrival.

"Right now I don't put a lot of credence in my instincts."

He stopped, his boots halting in the dusty drive and she kept on a few steps until she realized he wasn't with her anymore. She looked over her shoulder at him. His eyes flashed at her. "And I've done something to…not earn your trust? Is that it?"

He had her there. And yesterday's kiss…she couldn't blame him for that either. She'd wanted it as much as he had. Not that they'd talk about it. No way.

"I'm cautious, then," she responded, as they reached the steps. "Very, very cautious."

"So can Sam come with me or not?"

She left him in the doorway taking off his boots. "I'm still thinking," she said. She'd already made up her mind that Sam could go, but she wasn't going to let Luke think he'd won so easily.

Just as they were finishing the meal, a cloud of dust announced an approaching car. They both looked out the window and Emily heard Luke's heavy sigh. "Who is it?"

"My sister, Liz."

"The rhubarb sister."

He smiled at her summary. "Yes, that's the one." Emily watched as he checked his watch and tapped his foot. "Dammit, she's got perfect timing," he muttered.

Liz parked the car in the shade of a tree and Emily felt the strange, nervous feeling she'd had yesterday meeting Joe. As though she was an imposter, a tag-along.

"I'm sorry, Emily. I think the family is curious about you, and you've been put under the microscope."

"Why would they do that?"

Luke plopped his hat on his head. "Because you're not the matronly housekeeper they expected. Because you're staying here. Because you're young and pretty." He sighed. "Because people who are married think that everyone else in the world should be married, and they feel free to stick their noses in."

Emily opened her mouth and then closed it again, unsure of how she was supposed to react to that little tidbit. It wasn't the meddling that shook her—she half expected that. It was the *young and pretty* part. She was only twenty-eight but there were days she felt ancient. And pretty...she'd been living in T-shirts and yoga pants for so long that she forgot what it was like to feel pretty.

She wouldn't dream of admitting such a thing to Luke, though. Surely his family wasn't putting the cart this much before the horse. "Married?" The thought was preposterous, and she laughed. Even if she did want to get married—which she didn't—she'd only known Luke for a few days.

He raised his right eyebrow until it nearly disappeared beneath his hat. "Ridiculous, isn't it? But I'll bet my boots Liz is here to check you out. She'll have some good excuse. But don't worry, she means well. This should be the end of it. You can thank the Lord that I don't have more sisters to interfere."

With that he went outside to greet Liz.

Liz came towards the house, carrying a blond-headed baby on her hip and with two more youngsters trailing behind. Emily bit down on her lip. She was an object of curiosity now. Yesterday's longing for siblings and a close-knit family dissipated as she realized that intimacy also meant interference. The last thing she wanted was to be scrutinized. Judged. And to come up short.

"What brings you out, Liz?" Emily heard him call out and

closed her eyes. She could do this. Liz would never know how Luke's voice gave her goose bumps or how they'd kissed until they were both out of breath. Emily fluffed her hair, smoothed her fingertips over her cheeks, and let out a calming breath.

Luke met his sister in the yard. The twin girls took off running across the lawn, burning off some stuck-in-the-car energy.

"Strawberries," Emily heard the woman say. "I brought out a flat of strawberries."

"I'm in the middle of haying. When would I have time for strawberries?"

They'd reached the porch and Emily stood just inside the screen door of the house, wanting to scuttle away but knowing how that would look—as though she was running from something. Hiding. She had nothing to hide.

"Joe told us you've finally got some help. It's about time, Luke. Joe said she's very pretty, too. You've been holding out on us, brother."

"No big surprise, Nosy Nellie. Cait put the request in at the agency, after all. You can't fool me."

Emily's cheeks flamed as Liz looked up and suddenly realized Emily was standing behind the screen door. For a second, Liz got a goofy look on her face as she realized she'd been caught. Then she replaced the look with a wide smile.

"Joe was right. You are pretty. I'm Liz, Luke's sister."

Good heavens, was everyone in Luke's family so forthright?

"Berries are in the trunk, Luke. Be a good brother."

Luke's jaw tightened as Liz smiled and adjusted the weight of the baby on her hip. Emily looked to him for guidance, but he gave none. Emily couldn't stand to be impolite, so she opened the door. "Come on in. We were just having lunch. Come have some cobbler."

Liz swept in and Emily heard Luke's boots tromp off down

the steps. First Joe and now Liz. The family obviously thought there was more to the arrangement than a simple trading of services. Which there wasn't. Much. Emily wondered how fast the telephone wires would burn up if Liz knew that they'd kissed yesterday.

"Don't mind Luke," Liz admonished, nosing around the kitchen. "He's always a bear in haying season. No time to call his own, you know? Not the biggest conversationalist either."

Emily was tempted to set Liz straight on that. Last night and just a few moments ago Luke had managed to hold his own quite well in the conversation department. She wondered how he managed that. He seemed to say a lot, but none of it really told her anything. Except that he'd been left in charge of the family at a young age.

But she did not want to open that can of worms with Luke's sister. She wasn't a busybody and knew exactly how awful it was to have people pry into her situation. She would keep the conversation impersonal. "Rain's coming, Luke said."

Great job, Em, she thought. First words she spoke and she was parroting the forecast? Perhaps she could have come up with something slightly more inspired.

Liz nodded. "He'll work until dark tonight, I expect. Good to get the first cut in though. What do you think of the house?"

Emily busied herself fixing a bowl of cobbler and ice cream for Liz. "It's charming. Much nicer than the cookie cutter houses in the city."

Liz nodded. She sat at the table and perched the baby on her knee, bouncing her a little and making the little girl giggle. "I think so, too. Luke's done some work to it since taking it over, but for the most part it looks just like it did when we were growing up. Of course, I'm living in town now. And I've got the little ones to keep me busy."

Luke came back in, carrying a wooden flat filled with boxes of crimson strawberries. "I think the twins have made a new friend," he said dryly.

Emily and Liz went to the window. Sam and Liz's blond girls were racing through the yard, playing what appeared to be a rousing game of tag.

"It's good for Sam. He hasn't spent much time with friends since…"

She stopped. Since the divorce. Since there was no longer any money for playgroups and preschool.

"He'll have to come play with the twins while you're here. It'll get them out of my hair," Liz offered freely.

Another tie to break later? Emily wasn't sure it was a good idea. But then she balanced it against Sam being alone here in an unfamiliar place and no children to play with. "That might be nice."

"Call anytime." Liz replied, putting the baby down on the floor. The little girl rocked back and forth for a minute before setting off at a steady crawl. "You and Luke could come over for dinner."

"Liz," Luke warned, and Emily had to look away. It was such an overt bit of matchmaking that she squirmed in her chair.

"What? Look, both Cait and I are thrilled you have some help at last. That's all. And Emily doesn't know a soul besides you. And we all know what great company you are."

He raised an eyebrow at her.

"I'm heading back out. The boys are going to wonder where I am. Emily, tell Sam I'll take him out with me another time. He should enjoy the girls while they're here." He put his plate in the dishwasher and cut himself a massive slice of apple cake. "For the road," he said, flashing a quick grin.

She nodded and walked with him to the door.

"Are you sure you're okay with my sister?" he asked quietly, pausing and resting his palm against the frame.

Emily forced a small laugh. "You have work to do. I'll be fine."

"She's meddling. Thinking that this is more than it is."

That should have relieved her but didn't. Would it be so awful for them to think that he liked her, for heaven's sake? Not that she wanted him to, but was it incomprehensible that he might? "Don't worry about it. And it's good for Sam to have playmates for an hour or so. He's been lonely." She paused. "Are you really going to work until dark?"

His gaze plumbed hers for a long moment. It was a simple question but brought with it a picture of how the evening would unfold…Sam in bed, darkness falling, Luke coming to the house in the twilight. All of it played out in her mind as she gazed up into his eyes. How did he feel about coming home to her at night? Was she an intrusion? A complication? Or welcome company, as he was to her, despite his sometimes prickly ways?

"Probably close to it," he finally answered. "We'll go until it starts to cool off, then there are chores here to see to. You and Sam should eat without me. Just fix me a plate."

There wasn't any reason for her to feel disappointed, but she did. After only a few days she'd gotten used to seeing him during meals. Company, whereas before mealtime had meant an empty space at the head of the table.

"I'd like to make a run into town for sugar and pectin. Anything you need?"

He shook his head. "Not that I can think of. Thanks for asking, though." He started off but turned around again. "Don't let Liz needle you into anything," he warned. "Cait's the bossy sister, but Liz has a way of getting what she wants without you even knowing how."

CHAPTER SEVEN

As EMILY WENT back inside, three sweaty heads ran past her into the house.

"Whoa, slow down!" Liz called from the kitchen, laughing as the children scrambled in demanding a snack. The baby was heading for the stairs, and, without a second thought Emily picked her up, breathing in the scent of baby powder and milk. She closed her eyes for a moment, enjoying the feel of the weight on her arm, the smell that was distinctly baby. Sam had left those baby days behind him long ago. Emily had always hoped the time would be right to have another, but it had never worked out. Now she was a little glad it hadn't. She couldn't imagine being responsible for two precious lives in her current circumstances. Knowing she would probably never have any more caused a bittersweet pang in her heart. Being a single mom was tough. She knew she wouldn't deliberately grow her family without being in a secure relationship. And after the crumbling of her marriage, she never intended to go down that road again. Still, it was hard to say goodbye to those dreams.

As she opened her eyes, blue eyes reminiscent of Luke's stared up at her and she smiled. "Let's find your mama," she murmured, and settling the baby on her hip, she entered the kitchen to find Liz mixing up lemonade and three expectant faces watching.

Liz looked so comfortable that it reminded Emily that this was Liz's childhood home. Emily was the trespasser here and she felt it acutely as she watched Liz add sugar to the lemonade then open the correct drawer for a wooden spoon. Emily envied the other woman her level of comfort with, well, everything. And yet she had to admit she was drawn to Liz's breezy ways.

"Out on the porch with you three," Liz admonished, filling three plastic cups with the drink. "One cookie each. No sneaking."

When the kids were settled on the verandah she came back to the kitchen. "Thanks for grabbing Alyssa," she said, taking the bundle from Emily's arms. "The stairs, right? It's always the stairs."

Emily couldn't help but laugh. Liz might be a bulldozer but she was a pleasant one, and it had been a long time since Emily'd had a mom-to-mom visit with anyone. She'd been too busy coping to realize she was lonely.

Compared to Luke's reticence, Liz was bubbly and open. "How is it you are so different from your brother?"

"What do you mean?" Liz asked, grabbing her purse and taking out a biscuit for the baby to gnaw on.

"Luke's so..."

Emily struggled for the right word, thinking of how Luke looked at her and seemed to get to the heart of any matter with a few simple words. Liz's keen gaze was on her now.

Instantly Emily recalled the kiss and the way he'd cupped her neck confidently in his palm. "Intense."

"Luke's too serious, but I can't blame him. It's a wonder he didn't disown the two of us." She flashed a smile that hinted at devilry. "Oh, Cait and I gave him awful trouble."

"Surely your parents..."

"Oh, this was after Mom died and Dad had to be put in the

care home. Luke was different before that happened. Always running with his guy friends, you know?"

Care home?

Luke had said so little about his upbringing. Now the bits and pieces were starting to come together. Luke had said he'd been responsible for his sisters and the farm at an early age. She tried to imagine one parent dying and the other incapacitated. What an ordeal they must have gone through. "How old were you?"

"Luke was twenty. Cait was almost seventeen and I was fifteen. Old enough to know better, really. But at that age — when you're a teenager it's 'all about me', you know? We were still in high school."

Emily did know. But she also knew that Luke would have put himself last, making sure everyone was looked after ahead of himself. She imagined him waiting up for them at night, perhaps pacing the floor with lines of worry marring his forehead. Had those days put the shadows she saw in his eyes? "And Luke?"

Liz frowned. "He didn't tell you any of this?"

"Not much. Why would he? I've only been here a few days, Liz. We haven't had heart-to-hearts."

She smiled, but once the words were out she knew they weren't exactly true. Maybe not baring of souls, but she'd told him more about her marriage than she'd told anyone. They'd had moments of closeness—up to and including the kiss that had nearly melted her socks. Not that she'd admit that to his sister.

Liz dipped into her cobbler, holding the spoon in the air. "Well, Luke should be the one to tell you, not me."

"Luke isn't exactly big on social chitchat," Emily replied, but Liz just laughed.

"He does tend to be on the serious side. You ask him,

Emily. Maybe he'll talk to you. He never talks to either of us."

Maybe Luke was just a private person, Emily thought, but didn't say. Liz was his sister. She had to know him better than most. And she did feel a little odd, talking about him when he wasn't here. As curious as she was, Liz was right. This was something Luke should tell her himself. If he ever did.

"Joe said there's something going on between you."

Emily's back straightened, pulled out of her thoughts by Liz's insinuation. The camaraderie she'd begun to feel trickled away as she remembered Luke's warning. Liz was here to check her out, and the last thing she wanted was to be judged. "You are direct, aren't you?"

Liz raised her eyebrows. "Luke's our brother. We love him. We want him to be happy."

"And that's not with me." Of course not. Emily was not a brilliant prospect in anyone's book. She was damaged goods. She didn't even have a long-term plan.

Emily went to a cupboard and found a large mixing bowl and began stemming the first box of berries. She didn't like that she'd been the topic of conversation around the family water cooler.

"I didn't say that, you did."

The berries flew from one hand to the other and pinged into the stainless-steel bowl as Emily removed the stems. "I'm a single mother with a very small income."

"Money isn't what Luke needs." Liz's voice held a tinge of condemnation. "After what Joe said, I thought maybe you realized that. I guess I was wrong."

Emily's hands fell still. She had always considered that the outside world saw only the surface. That people looked at her and automatically categorized her in little columns of pluses and minuses. Lately she was pretty sure there were more minuses than pluses. Now she wondered if that was simply her own insecurity talking. "What does Luke need?" she asked quietly, picking up another berry but plucking off the stem at a more relaxed pace.

Liz brought another box to the side of the sink. "A companion."

Emily dropped the berry in the bowl. Luke was barely thirty. He didn't need a companion. He needed a wife and partner, and she wasn't up for applying for either position. "Then he should get a dog."

Liz laughed at her dry tone. "Fine, then. He needs a helping hand. Someone willing to share the load. He's been carrying it by himself for a long time. Not that he's ever complained. Someone should shake him up a bit. Why not you?"

A helpmate. Emily knew that was what Luke's sister was getting at and it made her pause. That's what she'd tried to be for Rob and it had blown up in her face. "I'm not interested in that," she informed Liz. "Nothing against your brother. He's very nice. But I'm not looking for a boyfriend or husband. I rely on myself now, not someone else."

Liz looked at her speculatively. "No one said you didn't."

But Emily knew that's what it would mean. She had built her whole existence around someone else. Rearranging her life around Rob's schooling and then his job. Staying home with Sam. Looking after everyone's needs and sacrificing her own. It had little to do with the type of work, she realized, but with the principle behind it. How long had she been Rob's wife, Sam's mother? How long had it been since she'd been plain Emily Northcott, woman?

"Liz, I appreciate that you want your brother to be happy. But surely you can see how ridiculous it is to be discussing this. There are no romantic notions. I work for him."

"If you say so," Liz replied, but Emily knew by her deliberately casual tone that she wasn't convinced. And why should she be? It wasn't exactly true. Emily thought about Luke far too often throughout the day and then there was the kiss. She ran her tongue over her lips, remembering the taste of him there. Knowing it wasn't what she wanted and yet dying to know if he would do it again.

"Either way, can we be friends?" Liz's sandy-colored ponytail bobbed as she reached beneath the cupboard for a colander to wash the berries, completely oblivious to Emily's quandary.

Friends? The request came as a surprise after being grilled about Luke. But an offer of friendship was hard to resist. She'd felt so disconnected in recent months. All of her friends were 'before divorce' friends. There'd been no money or time for cultivating new relationships since. Liz was only looking out for her family. Emily could hardly fault her for that. If she didn't feel so uncomfortable, she might have admired her for it.

Liz reached for the teakettle and filled it with water. "Come on, Emily," she invited. "Let's have a cup of tea and a gab. The kids are playing and Luke's going to be gone for hours. With the little ones underfoot I don't get out much either. What's the harm?"

What was the harm, indeed? Emily couldn't hold out against the temptation of a social afternoon. She got out the teabags and put them on the counter. "He told me you'd bull-doze me, you know." But she smiled when she said it, holding no malice against Luke's vivacious sister. She would have done the same thing for her brother or sister, if she'd had one.

"Of course he did."

Emily lifted a finger in warning. "But leave off the match-making, okay? Luke's no more interested in me than…"

She had been going to say than I am in him, but she couldn't say the words because she *was* interested in him, more than she would ever admit.

"Matchmaking? Perish the thought." Liz affected an

innocent look so perfectly that Emily found herself grinning back. "Listen," Liz continued, getting out spoons. "Luke has always said he will never get married anyway. So nothing to worry about, right?"

"I'd like to make some jam out of these berries," Emily said to Liz, offering an olive branch as the kettle began to whistle, trying to ignore Liz's latest bombshell. Never get married? She forced her mind back to the present. "Where's the best place to shop for jars and pectin?"

For the next hour the baby napped, the kids played in the sunshine and Liz and Emily stemmed the remaining berries, chatting easily about lighter topics. But the whole time Emily thought of Luke and his past. She couldn't help wondering why he was determined to be alone. Had he had his heart broken? Was it any of her business to ask? If she did, would he answer? She couldn't help the sneaky suspicion that Liz's throwaway comment had been intended to do just that—make her wonder.

The farmyard was dark except for the light Emily saw coming from the machine shed. It was past ten o'clock and still Luke hadn't come in. He hadn't had any supper, either. She'd waited for him long after Sam had gone to bed, finishing up the last batch of jam and leaving it to set on the kitchen counter. She couldn't forget all that Liz had told her during their chat—and what she hadn't.

She carried a warm plate in her hands as she crossed the gravel drive. The man had to eat something. If he wouldn't come in, she'd take it to him.

She balanced the plate on one hand and opened the door to the shed. All that was visible of Luke as she entered was his legs. The rest of him was underneath her car. A long yellow cord disappeared along with the upper half of his body—a trouble light illuminating the dirty job of changing her oil.

Clanking sounds echoed on the concrete floor as he put down the filter wrench and oil began draining into the catch pan.

"Luke?"

At the sound of her voice he slid out from beneath her car, the sound of the creeper wheels grating loudly in the stillness. The rest of his legs appeared, then came his flat stomach, his broad chest and muscled arms and then his head—now devoid of hat, his hair dark with sweat in the oppressive heat of the shop. Her gaze fixed on his arms as he pushed himself up to sitting.

Emily felt a bead of perspiration form on her temple in the close atmosphere of the shop. Throughout the afternoon the heat had increased until the kids had dropped, sapped of their energy. It hadn't let up after sundown. Even the peepers were quiet tonight, and when the creeper came to a halt, the silence in the shop was deafening.

"What are you doing with my car?"

"Changing your oil. It looked like it'd been a while."

It had, but that wasn't exactly the point. "I…you…" She didn't quite know what to say that didn't sound grouchy and angry. Especially since she was both of those things. Part of it was the heat. But a bigger part was that he'd taken it upon himself to do this without even consulting her.

"You might have asked me first."

Luke shrugged. "It's just an oil change, Emily."

Pride kicked in. "And the cost of the filter, and the cost of the oil."

"If it means that much to you, I'll deduct it from your pay."

Her hand shook beneath the warm dinner plate. She didn't want to lose any of her precious paycheck right now. And if she were to lose any of it, she should be the one to say where it went.

"That really wasn't on my list of things to do with my first check, Luke." She was trying—and failing—to keep a quiver out of her voice. "It's been a long time since I had my own pay. I'd like to be the one to decide what happens to it. And besides, it's after ten o'clock. You've already spent the day outside while I was inside with Liz...."

Suddenly the lightbulb came on. "That's it, isn't it? You're avoiding me because you think Liz put a bug in my ear."

He couldn't meet her eyes. "What's on the plate?"

"I'm right!" Victorious, she let out a breath. "You can't stay out here all night, you know. And you can't avoid me forever. For what it's worth, Liz barely told me anything. You could have saved yourself the trouble."

Luke put on his most nonchalant expression. "Your oil needed changing and I wanted to do it for you. Now, are you going to share that plate or did you just bring it out here to torture me?"

He got to his feet, looking sexier than a man had a right to in dusty jeans, work boots and a grease-stained T-shirt, and she had the thought that he could change her oil or tune up her car any time.

She held out the plate. "You should have come in for supper—you've got to be exhausted. The car could have waited. I know you want to get the hay in." She tried a smile. "You have to make hay while the sun shines, I've heard."

"That's true," he said. "With this heat—we need to get it baled before the rain comes tomorrow. I'm guessing thunderstorms. And there is always the chance of hail."

"Then take a rest."

He reached for a rag and wiped his hands before taking the plate. His fingers were long and rough, with a half-healed scratch running the length of one. He made a living with his hands and hard work. There was something earthy about that and she found it incredibly attractive.

"Lasagna. And garlic bread." He stared at the contents of

the plate with undisguised pleasure. "My God, that smells awesome. Do you know how long it's been since I had lasagna?"

"That's a good thing, then?"

He went to a wheeled stool and sat down. "Oh, yeah, it's a good thing." The shop began to fill with the scent of spicy tomatoes and beef. "Pull up a pew, Emily."

There was little space to sit, so she perched on the edge of a homemade sawhorse. Luke cut into his lasagna with the side of his fork, took a bite, and closed his eyes. Emily smiled, pleased she'd made the extra effort. Luke was turning out to be a pleasure to cook for. "It was better, fresh," she apologized.

"You say that, but I doubt it," he remarked, biting into the garlic bread, flakes off the crust fluttering down to the plate. "It's perfect just the way it is. I didn't realize how hungry I was. You didn't bring any water, did you?"

"Oh! How could I have forgotten?" She reached into the pocket of her light sweater and produced a bottle of beer, so cold it was already sweating with condensation. "I thought you'd appreciate a cold one."

He stared at her as if she were a gift from the gods. "What?" she asked, smiling. "You're not difficult to read, Luke."

Well, not about food, she amended mentally. In other ways he was a definite puzzle. Emily considered for a moment that perhaps Liz's perspective on what happened and Luke's could be very different. Not that Liz had it easy. Losing a parent had to be devastating. But having to step into that role as Luke had…

Luke popped the top and took a long drink. "That is exactly what I needed." He sighed, swiping the final slice of bread along the plate to get the last of the tomato sauce. "Thanks for bringing it out. You didn't need to do that."

"It was kind of quiet in the house."

He nodded. "Yeah, it gets that way."

Emily looked down, studying her toes. Had Luke been lonely? Up until now she really hadn't thought about him living in the house all alone, but now she wondered how it must be to come home to it every day, with no one there to talk to or share the silence with. At least she had Sam.

She picked a wrench up off the tool bench and toyed with it, putting it down and picking up another. When she looked up at Luke she could tell he was gritting his teeth. He came forward and took the wrenches, placing them back on the pegboard. The whole bench was precisely arranged and Emily wondered where he inherited his penchant for neatness from. "Sorry," she murmured.

"It's all right." His voice sounded oddly strained. "I try to keep things organized so…so I can always find the size I need."

"Tools on pegboard and everything on lists." She had noticed Luke had a list for everything at the house. Phone numbers. Groceries. To-do tasks. She often did the same thing, but she thought it an unusual trait in a man. "You really are quite neat and tidy, Luke. For a guy." She attempted to lighten the strange tension that had come over the room.

"I'm a one-man show. Keeping organized saves me a lot of time," he explained. He finished putting the tools away reached for his beer, toying now with the bottle as he sipped. "You survived Liz's visit?"

"We had tea and stemmed strawberries."

"And talked about me."

Emily felt a flush creep into her cheeks. "My, don't we have an inflated opinion of ourselves."

He laughed, the sound filling the quiet shed and sending a tingle right through to her toes. Laughter had been another one of those things that had been missing for a long time. Something that slipped away so innocuously that she hadn't realized she'd missed it until hearing it again.

"Liz was sticking her nose in. If Cait didn't have a newborn at home, she would have been here, too. Be thankful they didn't tag-team you. You wouldn't have stood a chance."

Emily stared at him. He was smiling as though it was a big joke. "So it's funny that I was put under the microscope today?"

He lowered the bottle slowly. "I forgot. You don't have brothers and sisters. It's what they do. We're born to aggravate each other. I guess I'm just used to it."

"Well she wasn't aggravating *you* today, was she?" Emily's back straightened. Granted, she'd had a nice visit with his sister, but Luke didn't know that. For all he knew he'd thrown Emily to the wolves and he was relaxed as could be, smiling like a fool.

His smile slid from his lips though when she fired that question at him. "What exactly did Liz say to you, Emily?"

"Worried?" She asked it in an offhand manner, but the smile from earlier was gone. "She didn't say much. She mentioned you looking after her and Cait and how they'd been holy terrors. But really, that was all."

Luke seemed to relax, turning the bottle in his fingers. "And she said I should ask you about the rest."

The bottle stopped turning.

"Why don't you tell me about your dad, Luke?"

"There's nothing to tell." His voice was hard and his knuckles went white on the bottle.

"He's in a special-care home, right?"

His head snapped up and his blue gaze flashed at her. "Liz has a big mouth."

"Then make me understand what makes you so different from your sister. Because I'm guessing it had to do with the fact that you had to leave your childhood behind in a hurry to take over this farm."

Emily went to him and put a hand on his arm. "Please,

Luke. I shared bits of my story with you. Can't you do the same? Maybe talking about it will help."

"All the talking in the world won't change things," he bit out.

"But it might make you feel less alone," she reasoned. "I know I felt better after talking to you. What happened to your father?"

It was quiet for several seconds and Emily didn't think he was going to answer. But then his voice came, low and raspy, as if the words were struggling to get out.

"Dad had been acting weird for a while. We'd all noticed it, but after Mom died…it was clear there was more to it than simple stress forgetfulness. It wasn't until he nearly burned down the house making eggs in the middle of the night that we couldn't ignore it any more."

"What happened? What was wrong with your father?"

"Early-onset Alzheimer's. Dad's been in a care home since. Over the years it's got progressively worse. Not so much at first. Sometimes the fog would clear and we had good visits, you know? We could talk about the farm, the girls, my mom. But those times got fewer and farther between and lately… he's really gone downhill. I don't expect he's got much time left."

Emily remembered the pictures on the old radio in the living room. The first day, she'd seen Luke's face turn sad as he looked at the picture of his parents. The bedroom upstairs, with its faded doilies and chenille spread, looking lost and abandoned…she'd bet now that no one had slept there since his father had been put in care. And he had given it to her. She felt a little weird about that, but honored, too. What a heart-breaking decision to have to make about your one remaining parent.

"Liz mentioned you having power of attorney. That means the decision fell to you, didn't it?"

He lifted tortured eyes to hers. "Yes. As well as the day-to-day running of the farm, and looking after the girls."

"But surely they were grown enough to look after themselves..."

Luke laughed, but it was laced with pain. "Cooking, laundry, cleaning, yes. But at fifteen and nearly seventeen, they needed guidance. I was twenty. My prized possession was my truck. I wasn't ready to be a parent to two hormonal teenage girls. I wasn't that much older than they were and I was trying to keep them from making mistakes. Trying to make sure they finished school, had opportunities, you know?"

"And so you sacrificed yourself."

"What else could I have done? And look at them. They graduated, got jobs, met fine men and started families. You can imagine what a relief that is. Think if it were Sam."

He'd been taking on responsibility all his adult life. And she'd been whining about her problems yesterday. Luke had been so understanding. More than understanding—caring.

She had been in danger of caring right back, and this new knowledge touched her, making her respect him even more. Making her grieve a little bit for the young man who had had to grow up so quickly. "And all this while you grieved for your parents."

His eyes shone for a few moments until he blinked.

"What did you give up, Luke? You put the girls first, so what dreams did you put aside for later?"

Luke put the bottle beside the empty plate and placed his hands on his knees. "It doesn't matter now."

"I think it does. You were twenty, carefree and with your life ahead of you. That must have been cut short..."

"I worked on the farm for a year, but I'd planned on going to college. I wanted to study genetics so I could play with our breeding program. The idea of going away for a while was exciting. Even after Mom died, I only planned to stay a year to help and then I'd be off. But as things progressed with Dad, I knew I couldn't leave. My responsibility was to the family, and to abandon them would have been the height of selfishness."

He gave her a knowing look. "You know as well as I do that you put family first. You'd do it for Sam. You're doing it for him now by making a life for him. But Emily, don't give up on your dreams either. You give up on them and you'll end up old and bitter like me."

Luke got up from his stool, worry lines marring his tanned brow. He reached out for her arm, but seemed to remember the state of his hands and pulled back. Emily felt the connection just the same as if he'd touched her.

She met his gaze. The connection seemed to hum between them every time their eyes met, but she would not shy away from eye contact. She was stronger than that. "You are not old and bitter," she whispered.

"Em..."

She swallowed. Luke was standing in front of her car now, his thumbs hooked in the front pockets of his jeans. For a moment she remembered what it had been like when he'd stepped forward and kissed her, so commanding and yet gentle. There could be no more repeats of that. He was right. She couldn't give up on her dreams, even if right now that meant doing the right thing for Sam.

"Why don't you go back and get your pharmacy degree?"

She pondered the idea for a moment. "It's not what I want anymore. I have Sam now and want to be close to him. Going to school and trying to support us...he'd be in daycare more than out of it."

"What about online learning?"

The idea was interesting. "Maybe. But not pharmacy. Not now." She smiled at him. "Priorities change."

He smiled back. "Don't I know it?"

Her heart took up a strange hammering, a persistent tap like a Junebug hitting a screen door time and time again.

"Thank you for telling me, Luke. I know it couldn't have been easy."

"It wasn't. But you were right. I do feel better, I think. Liz and Cait have different memories than I do. In some ways that is good. But it's hard talking to them about it. I don't want them to feel responsible for anything, and I think they will if I let on how hard it was."

"Would you do it again?"

It was a loaded question, and one Emily had asked herself often since the disintegration of her marriage. Would she marry Rob again, knowing what she knew now? But then she thought of the good times, and about Sam, asleep in his room with the June breeze fluttering the curtain and the moon shining through the window. Nothing could take away the love she had for her boy. She knew her answer. What was Luke's?

CHAPTER EIGHT

LUKE LEANED BACK against her bumper. What in the world had possessed him to talk to Emily this way? He never opened up to anyone, not even his sisters who had been with him all the way. He kept to himself, and that was how he liked it. And then Emily had blown into his life and turned everything upside down.

She had him talking. That was more of a surprise than his reaction to her. If he wasn't careful, she'd have him wishing for all kinds of things he'd stopped wishing for years ago.

But her question stayed with him, and he looked at her, perched on the sawhorse, her cheeks flushed from the heat and her hair mussed from running her hand through it too many times. Would he do it again the same way? Sacrificing what he'd wanted to look after his sisters?

"Of course I would. They'd lost both their parents. They needed guidance and support. Who else would have stepped in?"

"What about support for you, Luke?"

Damn her eyes that seemed to see everything.

"I could say the same for you, Emily. Who is supporting you now?" She opened her mouth, but he cut her off. "Don't bother, I know the answer. No one. You're going it alone, too. What about your parents? Any other family?"

"I want to do this on my own. I need to. I know they are there if I need them."

"And then there's Sam."

Her eyes blazed and her back straightened. "Everything I do is for Sam!"

Luke smiled indulgently. "Calm down, I know that. Just as you get why I did what I had to for the girls. Choosing myself first would have been self-centered, especially when they needed me so badly."

"You're a good big brother," she murmured. "Do the girls realize how much you gave up for them?"

He shrugged. "Does it matter? They are healthy and happy and I am happy for them." He fought against the sinking feeling in his chest. He was happy for them with their strong marriages and beautiful children. He was thrilled they both had clean bills of health. He also knew that all three of them couldn't be so lucky. Not that he would wish their father's affliction on either of them. Of course not. But it stung just the same, seeing them with their picture-perfect lives and knowing the same wasn't in the cards for himself.

It was a good thing Emily's job only lasted until September. He would manage again after that. He'd put up with Cait coming and going and fussing. Getting closer to Emily wasn't an option, not when he'd just have to push her away again.

"That's all I want for Sam, too," Emily said softly. "He's essentially lost his father and his home and any place he's belonged. Kids do better in consistent environments. Yanking him from place to place isn't good for him. This is kind of like summer vacation for him. I know I've got to figure some things out and find us a more permanent situation."

"You're a good mother, Emily. Did you see his face today at the garden? He's having the time of his life. He's enjoying the outdoors, the freedom. And for all Liz's meddling, the twins are good girls. He could do worse for playmates. You're doing the right thing."

"I don't want him to get in your way, though. I know you have a farm to run. This thing about the tractor...don't feel obligated."

Luke blinked in surprise. What was it about the tractor? Was she worried he'd get hurt? Or did she just not trust him with her son? "Did I give you the idea I didn't like children, Emily?"

"Well, yes, kind of." A mosquito buzzed in front of Emily's face and she brushed it away. He couldn't tell if she were blushing or not because the heat kept her cheeks flushed, but he saw her shift her weight on the sawhorse and wondered.

"You weren't excited about the baby. In fact, you lamented the fact that the newest member of the family was another girl, and came right out and said you didn't want a family. Liz's kids were here today and you barely gave them a glance. You can't honestly say you want him underfoot," she challenged. "He would get in your way."

Luke stilled, feeling as if he'd been struck. Was it that obvious? Did Cait and Liz feel the same way? That he didn't care about their kids? He had kept his distance because it was a constant reminder of how different his life was. But he hadn't considered that they might feel slighted. Unloved. Regret sliced through him.

And he would die before explaining why to Emily. It was bad enough he'd said as much as he had.

"I never meant to give that impression. Of course there are times he needs to be at the house, but there's also no reason why he can't come with me now and again. He can play with Liz's kids. The Canada Day celebrations are soon. There'll be lots of activities for the kids. Has he ever ridden a horse?"

She shook her head.

"I'm not very good at showing my feelings, Emily. That's all. Don't take it personally."

"It is lovely here. The house is a joy and I'm loving the fresh air and freedom of it. I think Sam is, too. If he gets in the way, just tell me, Luke. He's my son, not yours. My responsibility. You don't need to feel like you have to...whatever."

Her words shouldn't have stung but they did. Yes, Sam was her son, and a reminder that Luke would never have one of his own. He would never burden a family the way he'd been burdened.

"Just enjoy the summer, Emily. Think about what you want to do when it's over. Just because I had to give up my dreams doesn't mean you have to give up yours."

The fluorescent lights hummed in the silence.

"I should go in, it's getting late."

Luke cleared his throat. "Your oil is definitely drained. I'll put on the new filter and be behind you in a few minutes." He boosted himself away from the hood of the car and reached for a plastic-wrapped cylinder on the workbench.

"Luke?"

"Yeah?"

"Could you show me how to do that sometime? How to change my oil and stuff? I'd like to be able to do it for myself."

After all they'd talked about tonight, the simple request was the thing that touched him most. She was so intent on being independent. And she trusted him. For some weird reason, she trusted him and it opened something up inside him that had been closed for a very long time.

"Next time we get a rainy day, I promise," he said. "Now get on up to the house. It's after eleven. And morning comes early."

"Yes, boss," she replied, but the tension from her face

had evaporated and she smiled as she picked up his plate and empty bottle. She paused by the door. "Luke?"

He looked up from his position on the creeper. "Em?"

"Thanks for the talk. I'll see you in the morning."

She scuttled out the door, but Luke leaned his head back, resting it on the grill of the car and closing his eyes.

Emily had snuck past almost all of his defenses tonight. And if he wasn't careful, she'd get through them all. And then where would they be?

Curses. Emily put one foot after the other going back to the house in the dark, the echo of a wrench sounding behind her in the stillness. His last word to her had been the shortened version of her name and it had sent a curl of awareness through her. She entered the dark house, left the dishes in the kitchen and felt her way up the steps, using the banister for guidance. In her room she paused, thinking about what had been said and what hadn't. Luke had held back at times, and she wondered why. Now she was more aware than ever that the two bedrooms were only short steps away from each other. She'd be beneath her sheet tonight, listening to the breeze in the trees, and he'd be just on the other side of the wall, doing the same thing.

Damn.

She could do this. She refused to fall for Luke Evans. Maybe they'd reached a new understanding of each other tonight, but that was all. She had to put Sam first, and that didn't include fooling around with the boss. What she needed to do was appreciate what was good about the situation. All the great things about living on a farm could be theirs for the next few months.

Then there was sitting across from Luke at the table, seeing his face morning, noon and night, washing his clothes, smelling the scent of his soap as she hung up his damp towel in the morning. She swallowed. That was the problem. She didn't want to be attracted to him, but she was. She couldn't not be. He was one-hundred-percent strong, virile male, hardworking and honest.

But attraction and acting on it were two very different things. As she lay in the dark, listening for him to return to the house, she thought about what he'd said about school. There was merit there. Perhaps she could talk to her parents after all. It would do Sam good to have family around him more as she got back on her feet. And with her summer's earnings she could buy a laptop and take a few courses.

She was still waiting and planning when she finally drifted off to sleep.

Luke squinted up at the sky, watching the broad roll of clouds balling up in the west. They were still a long way away, but as he wiped the sweat trickling off his brow, he knew they were thunderheads. The forecast had been right for once, though he wished it hadn't. He turned the wheel of the tractor, making one last pass with the rake, watching the Orrick boys work the baler. Hail would wreck what was cut, making it good for nothing. They'd finish, by God, before the rain came. They'd finish if it killed him.

It was a race against time and no one stopped for a lunch break as they worked, dirt mixing with sweat on their brows in the sweltering waves of heat. The thunderheads piled on top of each other, reaching to massive heights and creeping their way eastward to Brooks, Duchess and everywhere in between. He thought of Emily and Sam back at the house. He should have brought his cell. He had no doubt Em could handle a thunderstorm, but he would have liked to hear her voice, to make sure she wasn't out somewhere when the storm hit. To ask her if she'd brought in the hanging baskets. If Sam was okay.

He shook his head. When had he started to care so much? How was it that she snuck into his thoughts no matter where he was or what he was doing?

The thunder was just starting to grumble when the last bale was rolled. James and John Orrick took off their caps and wiped their foreheads, looking up at the sky. The sun still beat down relentlessly but it was coming. There was no sense denying it. "Just in time," James commented, putting his cap back on his head.

Luke scanned the field. The surface of the huge round bales would protect the hay on the inside. Nothing would be lost today. As long as it was just a thundershower. Tornadoes weren't common, but they happened now and again. And if he'd learned anything over the last nine years, it was that you simply had to accept the weather and roll with the punches. He thought of Emily and Sam again. They would be safe in the house. But he wanted to be home with them. To know they were there—warm and dry and safe. No matter how much he hadn't wanted the responsibility of them, he felt it anyway. It would have been easier if it felt like a burden, but it didn't. It felt right, and that was what had kept him up at night.

"Might as well head in, boys. Go home and shut your windows."

Everyone laughed, but it was a tight sound. The air had changed, bringing a shushing sound with it. It was a restless sound, like the wind holding its breath.

They made their way back to the farmyard. The hanging baskets were off the hooks and tucked under the porch roof, their leaves limp in the midday heat. So Emily was aware of the impending storm. Luke's stomach growled since he'd missed lunch, but at the same time a whicker sounded from the corral; Bunny and Fred and Caribou were still outside, nervous just like anyone else at the change in the air. Luke thought about letting them out into the pasture, but then scanned the clouds. If there was hail, he wanted them to be indoors. He forgot about lunch and went to put them in the barn, secured them in their stalls and soothed them with pats and fresh water. Back at the house, all was quiet. Sam was sitting at the table with a coloring book, scribbling busily at a picture of one of the latest superheroes.

Emily appeared at the dining-room door, smiling but he could see she was nervous underneath the cheerful exterior. "You're back. Did you finish?"

"Just." He turned his head towards the door. "You took down the baskets."

"Hard to miss that change in the air. I hope it's not bad. I'd hate for hail to take out the garden. Everything's just starting to come along. Not to mention crops. Do you think it'll be bad, Luke?"

He shrugged. "I hope not, but it's out of my hands. The hay's baled and the horses are in. That's about all I can do. Maybe it'll miss us altogether."

The tension left her face at his reassurances. "I wasn't sure when you'd be in. I made you a sandwich and put it in the fridge."

Luke knew Emily had never been a farm wife, so how was it she seemed to know exactly what he needed and when? He washed his hands and sank into a chair as exhaustion finally crept in now that he'd stopped. He'd been going flat-out for days now and not sleeping well at night. He hadn't visited his father in two weeks and felt guilty about it. He thought of Emily far too often and felt guilty about that as well. There was nothing to do right at this moment, though, and it all seemed to catch up with him. He drank a full glass of cool, reviving water before biting into the thick sandwich of sliced ham and cheese. As he swallowed the last bite, she quietly put a slice of rhubarb pie at his elbow.

"Thank you, Emily."

"You're welcome."

There was a low rumble of thunder in the distance, and the leaves of the poplars twisted in the breeze. He took his dirty dishes to the sink. The hot breeze from the open window hit him in the face. He closed his eyes.

"Hey, Em? I'm going to lie down for a few minutes."

She came to the door, holding a red crayon in her hand. "Are you feeling all right?"

He smiled. "Just tired. It's this heat. It just saps you."

"Okay."

He went to the living room and sank on to the plush cushions of the sofa, hanging his stocking feet over the arm. He closed his eyes. He'd get up in a few minutes, a short break was all he needed. His breaths deepened as he thought of all the little things Emily did, lifting his burdens and doing it with a smile. She had made the house like a home again, with voices and laughter and delicious smells.

It was just like it used to be, he thought as he drifted off to sleep. Like when Dad came in from a tough day and Mom met him with a kiss and a cup of coffee...

Emily heard the deep breaths coming from the living room and her hand paused, the crayon a few inches from the paper. Luke was plain worn out. She'd seen it in the dark circles beneath his eyes and the tired way he'd sunk into his chair in the kitchen. She watched Sam color a comic-book character in his coloring book and exhaled, wishing the sultry air would clear. It was close, suffocating. The leaves on the trees tossed and turned now, restless in the wind coming before the storm. The weather was as unsettled as she was. Calm on the surface but churning inside.

Emily paced a few minutes, coming to stop at the door to the living room. She looked down at Luke's face, relaxed in sleep. The scowl he wore so often was gone and his lips were open just the tiniest bit. He had long eyelashes for a man. She hadn't realized it before, but watching him sleep gave her the chance to really examine his face. He snuffled and turned his head, revealing a tiny scar just behind his left ear.

How could she make it through two more months of this if she already felt the tugs of attraction after a handful of days? There had been no repeats of the kissing scene. Not even a glance or small touch. And still he was on her mind constantly. When she lay in bed listening to the frogs or when she was mixing up batter or taking clothes off the line. She replayed the kiss over and over in her head, remembering what it was like to feel desirable. To feel her own longings, emotions she'd thought quite dead and buried. She was starting to trust Luke. The world was not full of Robs. Deep down she'd always known it, but it was easier to think that than to face the truth.

Emily swallowed. A cold puff of air came through the windows, the chill surprising her. It didn't take a genius to figure it out. She hadn't been enough to make Rob happy, and she wasn't sure she could survive failing again. She was tired of apologizing for it. He had been selfish leaving when they might have worked it out. He hadn't appreciated what he had...and now she looked down at Luke. Luke, who was so handsome he took her breath away. Luke, who had kissed her in the kitchen with his wide, strong hands framing her face and who said thank you for everything.

She turned away from Luke's sleeping form. It was impossible she was even *thinking* such a thing. She shook her head. Didn't she need to get Sam settled and her life in order first? Of course she did. She couldn't lose sight of the goal. Self-reliance came first. She'd made a promise to herself and she meant to keep it. And a promise to Sam. To even think of indulging herself in what—an affair? Luke wasn't interested in a relationship. In kids. He'd made it clear when he'd talked to her about what she was going to do when she left the ranch. Even entertaining the idea was selfish—thinking of herself rather than of what was best for Sam in the long run.

Emily had been so caught up in her thoughts that she hadn't noticed the room growing dark. What had been distant rumbling was now persistent, grumbling rolls of thunder. A flash went through the room, like a distant camera flash, and seconds later the thunder followed. She hurried to check on Sam, who had put down his crayons and stared at her with wide eyes.

"Boomers comin'?"

"I think so, honey."

Sam's dark eyes clouded with uncertainty. Her boy tried to be brave and strong, but she knew he hated thunderstorms. "Don't worry, okay? We're snug as a bug here."

Sam slid from his chair as another flash of lightning speared the sky. "I need to close the windows, Sam. It's starting to rain and I don't want things to get wet. You can come with me if you want."

But he shook his head, his hair flopping. "I'll stay here. I don't wanna go upstairs. Hurry back, Mommy."

Emily darted from room to room, shutting windows against the angry raindrops beginning to fall. Upstairs in Luke's room, the window stuck. She pushed down on the slider, making progress, but only in half-inch increments. The wind blew back the curtains, twisting them in her face as she struggled with the swollen window frame.

Just as it slid into the groove a fork of lightning jutted out of the sky, lighting up the whole house—followed by an astounding, foundation-shaking blast of thunder. The burst was so violent her heart seemed to leap and shudder before settling again into a quick, shocked rhythm.

She heard Sam scream and raced out of Luke's room to the stairs. She skidded into the dining room—no Sam. Emily pushed a hand through her hair, forcing her breath to calm. The bang had frightened her, too. "Sam?" she called, as another lightning strike and clap of thunder reverberated through the house.

"In here."

Luke's gravelly voice answered her from the living room.

She found them huddled together in a great walnut rocking chair. Luke's feet were planted square on the floor, and a terrified Sam was cradled in his arms, his bare feet resting on Luke's thigh as he curled up in Luke's lap. The strong arms she couldn't forget being around her now circled her son securely and the chair rocked ever so slightly.

The sight did something to her heart. It confirmed what she'd sensed at the beginning—Luke was a good, caring man hidden by a crusty exterior. He wasn't telling Sam that being afraid was silly or making him buck up, that it was only a little storm. He was simply holding him, comforting him. Rain started coming down in torrents now, hammering on the roof and windows so loudly it made a vibrating hum. Luke's gaze met hers, calm and accepting. Whether or not it made sense, Emily knew in that moment that this was where they were meant to be. This was where they would both put themselves back together before moving on.

"Sam," she said gently, "Mommy's here now. It's okay."

The storm raged around them, echoing through the house. Sam shook his head and only burrowed deeper into Luke's shirt.

"It's okay, Emily. He's fine where he is."

Had she really accused Luke of not liking children? The way he held Sam was strong and caring and sent a slice through her heart as sharp as a fork of lightning. Had Sam been missing the presence of a man in his life? At first she had thought it was just Rob he missed. But she could tell he missed having a man to look up to.

She knew after a year of struggling that she could do this on her own. But there was something about having Luke in her life right now that somehow divided the burden.

A terrific crash sounded, not thunder but sharper and harder, and Emily sank into a nearby chair, her hands shaking. Lightning had hit something and she didn't have the courage to peer out the window and see what. She heard Luke murmur something reassuring to Sam as his toe kept the chair in motion, rocking and soothing. Her son whom she loved more than life itself. And the man who was proving that the shell she'd built around her heart wasn't as tough as she thought.

At the same time, the house went strangely quiet as the power went out. The fridge stopped its constant hum and the clock on the DVD player went dark.

"Looks like we'll be grilling tonight," Luke said easily.

After several minutes the storm made its way east. Emily looked over at Sam. His head had drooped and Luke smiled. "He fell asleep about five minutes ago," Luke said.

"I can move him…"

"Leave him. He's comfortable."

He had to stop being so nice. It only made things more impossible. "Luke…surely you can see the problem. He already trusts you…"

"If he does, why can't you?"

"It's not that simple." She kept her voice a low murmur, needing Sam to stay asleep. "What happens in August when we have to leave, Luke? When he has to say goodbye to you? And this ranch? If he gets too attached, how can I pull him away? How can I do that to him again?"

"He's a smart kid. He knows this is temporary…"

"He's only five." She dug her fingers into the arm of the chair.

"He already loves being here," Luke argued. "So whether

you go now or in a few months, you may have that to deal with anyway." He gave her a knowing look. "Or are we not talking about Sam here? I think it's you. You don't want to get attached to this place. Because you like it here."

"Of course I do…"

"And saying goodbye will be…"

She imagined driving away and watching Luke get smaller in her rearview mirror. After only a few days, she knew she'd miss him.

"I'm a big girl. I know how the world works."

"You sure do."

Sam let out a delicate snore. Luke's lips curved and then he lifted his head, sharing the smile with Emily.

Something clicked inside her. Suddenly it wasn't about protecting her heart from Luke anymore. He'd already breached the walls. She was in perilous danger of caring for him, truly and deeply caring.

She sat for a few moments, wanting to snatch Sam away from the security of Luke's arms, knowing it was foolish and petty. She should have foreseen she'd get in too deep.

But this job could give her the start she needed. She only had to keep the goal firm in her mind—a temporary retreat to regroup and then move forward. If she did that, it would all be fine.

She would enjoy every blessed minute she could, she decided. She'd be here when the beans ripened and the pea pods popped in the sunshine. Sam could maybe go for that horseback ride—maybe they both would. She could spend an hour on the porch with a paperback while Sam played.

When she looked back at Luke, his lips had dropped open as he dozed off, too. Seeing them sleeping together made her feel as though she was losing Sam, even as her head told her it was a ridiculous thought.

She had spent months worrying about the lack of a male

influence in Sam's life. Now that he had it, she wasn't sure she could resist the man—the real live cowboy, as Sam put it—who was putting stars in both their eyes.

CHAPTER NINE

FOR THE NEXT week Emily, Sam and Luke settled into a routine. Luke spent his days working the fields and Emily did the hottest work in the mornings. In the afternoon she ran errands or took time out to play with Sam, roaming the extensive yard looking for wildflowers and animal tracks. Luke made an effort to arrive for dinner and they all ate together. And as the sun sank below the prairie, Emily listened to the peepers and the breeze through the open windows of her bedroom. Luke was right next door and often she lay awake at night knowing the head of his bed was only a wall away. What was he thinking as his head lay on the pillow? There was a sense of comfort that came from knowing he was so close, but she wondered what to do with the attraction that kept simmering between them.

Because it *was* simmering. He hadn't touched her again. There hadn't been any more kisses. But the memory of the first kiss always seemed to hover between them, and every time she looked at him she felt the same jolt running from her heart down to the soles of her feet. It stood between them like an unanswered question. The only thing Emily could do was focus on her job. Feelings, attraction…it was all secondary right now. She had to keep her eye on the prize—self-reliance. She would need Luke's recommendation when she went job-hunting at the end of the summer, and she wouldn't do anything foolish to jeopardize it.

One mild evening Luke took Sam for a walk around the corral on Bunny's back, getting him used to the feel of the horse before letting Sam take the reins himself. After that, Sam was permanently smitten with both Luke and with the mare. It was all he talked about as he helped in the garden or dried the dishes, standing on a stepstool. He visited with Liz's twins one afternoon while Emily shopped for groceries. Emily had a look at the old record player and thought she might have a go at fixing it up. The cabinet was filled with old LPs. What would it be like to hear the scratchy albums again?

They all slipped into the routine so easily that it felt, to Emily at least, a little too real.

Then Luke came home with Homer.

At first Emily just heard the barking and she wrinkled her brow. Had a neighbor's dog strayed into the yard? Her heart set up a pattering, as she knew Sam would be paralyzed with fear. He'd never quite gotten over his fear of dogs since he'd nearly been attacked. She dried her hands on a tea towel and headed for the door.

Sam was making a beeline for the porch, his normally flushed cheeks pale. Emily scooped him up as Luke approached, holding a leash in his hand attached to a brown-and-white dog that limped behind.

Luke paused several feet away from the steps. Sam was clearly afraid of the new pup. It showed in the pallor of his face and how he clung to his mother.

"Sam, this is Homer."

No response. Luke's heart sank. He'd seen the dog weeks ago and had fallen in love. Oh, he knew that sounded ludicrous, but he had a soft spot for dogs and especially one like Homer, who needed a home so badly. But Homer had been in no shape to be adopted and in the hectic pace of haying season, it had gone to the back of Luke's mind. Until the veterinarian had called a few days ago. Luke had thought of Sam, too. He'd thought Homer could be a playmate. He hadn't thought about the boy being afraid.

"You don't have anything to fear from Homer," Luke said easily. He put his hand on Homer's back and the dog sat, his tongue hanging out happily. "He's the gentlest dog you'll ever meet."

Sam shook his head and clung to Emily even tighter. Luke noticed the shine of tears in her eyes and resisted the urge to sigh. He had to help the boy. Had to show him he didn't need to be afraid. He wasn't sure why, but he knew that it was important to help Sam overcome this hurdle. Maybe because he saw in Sam's eyes what he'd seen too often in his own— knowledge and understanding. Even at such a young age, Sam had been hurt and had grown—painfully—because of it. Luke couldn't fix that. But maybe he could make this better.

"We had an incident in the park last year," Emily said quietly. "Someone had their dog off leash and it started to go at Sam. I reached out and grabbed its collar." She looked down at Luke with liquid chocolate eyes. "He's been terrified ever since."

Homer whined and Luke heard distressed sounds coming from Sam's throat.

"Homer, hush."

Luke gave the firm order and the dog immediately quieted. He squatted down and put his hand on the brown-and-white fur. "Stay." He dropped the leash. Then he stood, went to Emily, reached out and touched Sam's back.

"Look at him now, Sam. Harmless as a flea." He spoke softly to the boy, knowing a gentle and steady touch was required. Sam obediently turned his head and looked at the mutt, whose tongue was hanging out in happy bliss as he panted.

Luke couldn't accomplish putting Sam at ease while he

had a death grip on his mother. "Come here, buddy," he said, and he lifted Sam right out of her arms and settled him on his hip. He half expected Sam to cry and reach for Emily, but he didn't. Knowing Sam trusted him did something to Luke's insides, something warm and expansive. Luke pointed at the dog. "Do you know what's special about Homer?"

Sam shook his head.

Luke looked over at Emily and smiled, hoping to thaw the icy wall that had suddenly formed around her. "Homer had an accident a while back. He's been at the vet's, because he was a stray and no one claimed him. A few weeks ago he was still wrapped up in bandages. You never saw a sorrier sight than that dog. He didn't even bark. He just looked up at me with his big, sad eyes."

He shifted his gaze to Sam, pleased that he had the boy's full attention. Sam's eyes were wide, listening to Luke retell the story. "Now he's healed up, but because he was hurt so badly, no one has given him a home." Luke paused, wondering if he should explain what fate would have befallen Homer had he not brought him home. "He isn't perfect, you see. But I think it doesn't matter if someone isn't perfect, don't you?"

Sam nodded. "Mama says everyone makes mistakes."

Luke swallowed. This was what he'd tried to avoid for so long, why he kept his nieces at arm's length. He was afraid of caring, and he'd been right. Holding Sam this way, hearing his sweet voice talk about his mama only reminded Luke of his vow to not have children of his own. How could he be so selfish, knowing he could pass his genes on to another generation? How could he have a family, knowing they might have to go through what he'd already suffered?

But the longing was there. It was there when he held Sam, and it was there when he looked at Emily, and if he wasn't careful it could have the power to break him.

He cleared his throat. "Dogs aren't that different from

people, you know. Give them a full belly and a little love and they're pretty contented."

Sam's shoulders relaxed and his gaze focused on Luke's face. Luke's gaze, however, fell on Emily. The ice in her gaze had melted and she was looking at him in a way that made his heart lift and thump oddly against his ribs. Lord, she was beautiful. Those big eyes that seemed to reach right in and grab a man by the pride. He realized he'd been holding his breath and staring a little too long, so he looked away and shifted Sam's weight on his hip.

"Homer won't hurt you. I promise. The biggest danger to you is that he might lick you to death." With an unprotesting Sam on his arm, he knelt before the dog. He stroked the fur reassuringly and Homer stretched a little, loving the attention. Still, Luke didn't force the issue, just let Sam watch his fingers in the dog's fur.

Sam's eyes were wide as he touched the soft coat. Soaking in the attention, Homer rolled over on to his back and presented his belly to be scratched.

That was when Sam noticed, and it all came together.

"He only has three legs!"

"Yep." Luke gave Homer's belly a scratch and the dog twisted with pleasure. "Doesn't slow him down much, though, does it? The vet told me he fetches tennis balls and who knows, maybe he can help me round up cattle if I can train him right. If you squat down like me, and hold out your hand, he can smell you. That's how you say hello."

Luke made Homer sit again and was beyond pleased when Sam followed his calm instructions. He balanced on his toes and held out his fingers, but when Homer moved to sniff he pulled them back.

Luke reassured him, wanting him to try again. They'd come this far. To stop now would mean two steps back. And Sam could do it. Luke knew he was just timid and that the worst of the fear was gone. Sam and Homer would be friends. He couldn't give the kid back what he'd lost, but he could give him this companion.

"Watch." He held out his hand and Homer gave a sniff and a lick. "Want to try again?"

He held out his fingers and Homer sniffed, licked and gave a thump of his tail.

"Give him this," Luke suggested, standing and reaching into his pocket. He took out a small dog biscuit and handed it to Sam. "Put it flat in your hand, and tell him to be gentle."

"H-Homer, gentle," Sam said, holding out his hand. Luke could see it trembled a bit, but Homer daintily took the treat and munched.

"See?"

"I did it!" Sam turned to his mother and beamed. "I did it, Mom!"

Emily smiled. "You sure did, baby," she replied. Homer barked and Sam jumped, his eyes wide again, but Luke chuckled. "That's just his way of saying thank-you," he said. He reached into his denim jacket and took out a rubber ball. "Homer, fetch," he commanded, tossing the ball, and the dog was up and off in a flash.

"Why don't you play fetch with him for a bit, Sam? Then I can talk to your mother."

Sam moved off with the dog and Luke looked up at Emily.

"I didn't know he was afraid."

"I wish you had asked, Luke. When I heard the barking, and saw Sam's face…"

"I'm sorry, Emily. Homer's been at the vet's for weeks and I couldn't stand to see him put down. Not when I could give him a good home. And I thought Sam would love him. Especially after all he's had to give up."

Was that a sheen of tears he detected in her eyes? His heart took up the odd thumping again.

"What you just did...that was great. Sam's been timid around dogs for months. Every time we meet a new dog, it's the same thing..."

Luke exhaled and smiled, until he heard the word *but*.

"But what happens when we leave, Luke? Homer is one more thing he will have to leave behind. Did you think of that?"

He hadn't, but he realized now he should have. "Take him with you."

But that was the wrong thing to say. "Take him with us? I don't know if he'd be welcome at my parents', and if Sam and I get an apartment...not everyone will accept pets. Then what happens when I'm gone to work and Sam is at school?"

Luke knew she was right. He climbed the steps and went to stand before her, needing her to understand. "Obviously I didn't think it through as well as I should have."

"I don't know how much more I can take away from him," she whispered, and he heard the catch in her voice.

He put his hand on her arm, feeling her warm skin beneath his rough fingers. "You are not taking anything away, Em. You give to him constantly. You give him love and acceptance and security. He is lucky to have you as a mother."

"You're just trying to get around me." She sniffled a little and looked away from him, but he put a finger under her chin and made her look back.

"Maybe." He felt the beginnings of a smile as he confessed. "If you'd seen Homer there, Em. He was skin and bones and bandages. Look what some love and attention accomplished. How could I just leave him there? I couldn't. I'm sorry for causing you problems, though."

"First me and Sam, now Homer. You do have a way of picking up strays, don't you?"

"Hey, you found me."

The sound of Sam's laughter drifted up over the porch and everything seemed to move in slow motion. Emily looked up into his eyes and he was helpless. "I guess I did," she murmured, and it was all he could do to keep from kissing her the way he'd been wanting to for days.

But what would it accomplish? Nothing had changed. And he wouldn't play games. It was bad enough his heart was getting involved. Acting on it was another matter entirely. It would get messy. People would get hurt. And he was kidding himself if he thought it was only Sam and Emily who'd pay the price.

Because ever since their arrival, *he*'d felt like the stray who'd been taken in. And he didn't like that feeling. He didn't like it at all.

They went to the Canada Day celebrations on the first of July and Emily finally met Luke's sister Cait and baby Janna. Unlike Liz and her bubbly nosiness, Cait was more reserved, with a warm, new-mother contented smile. Liz and her husband Paul were there with the girls, who tugged Sam along to the various games. They all ate cotton candy and hot dogs dripping with ketchup and mustard and as darkness finally fell, the three of them joined Cait, Joe, Liz, Paul and the kids on some spread-out blankets to watch the fireworks. It was impossible not to feel like a family. Like someone who belonged here. She knew it wasn't so, but it didn't stop the wishing. It would be foolish to imagine things were more than they seemed, but Emily wondered if some day she might find this somewhere, with someone.

The trouble was, she couldn't envision it at all. It was only Luke she saw in her mind and that fact bothered her more than she wanted to admit.

Emily sat cross-legged on the rough blanket, looking down

at Sam and watching his sleepy eyes droop while he valiantly struggled to keep them open. It was well past his bedtime, but he had wanted to stay and she didn't have the heart to say no. His head was cradled in her lap and she smoothed his hair away from his forehead as twilight deepened and the crowd gathered, waiting for the pyrotechnics show.

"He's tired."

Luke kept his voice low and spoke close to her ear, so close she felt the heat rise in her cheeks as the rest of her body broke out in goose bumps.

"He wouldn't miss this for the world."

"Neither would I."

Emily turned her head the slightest bit, surprised by how close Luke was when her temple nearly grazed his jaw. She knew he could be talking about the fireworks or visiting with neighbors or simply being there with his sisters and family. But Emily wanted to believe he meant being there with her and with Sam. How many times over the last week had they all been together and she'd felt the tug? A sense of déjà vu, knowing this had never happened before?

"Luke, I…" She didn't know how to tell him what was in her heart. There were times when she even felt guilty for taking a wage for the work she was doing. Not because what she did wasn't of value, but because she knew very well she was getting more than financial gain out of it. Sam was happy, she was happy, and she hadn't expected to be, not for a very long time.

There was a bang and the first jet of sparks flew upwards. Emily turned her head to the fireworks display as Sam sat bolt upright and exclaimed at the blue and purple cascade flowering in the sky. Emily heard Sam's name called and nudged him as Liz's twins gestured wildly for him to join them on their blanket just ahead. "Go on," she smiled. "You can watch with the girls. I'm right here."

Sam scooted up to the next blanket, leaving Emily alone with Luke.

Darkness formed a curtain and everyone's eyes were fixed on the dazzling display in the sky while Emily's heart thundered. Luke shifted on the blanket, moving behind her so that she could lean back against his strong shoulder to watch. She could smell the aftershave on his neck, feel the slight stubble of his chin as it rested lightly against her temple. One after another the explosions crested and expanded, a rainbow of colors, but all Emily could think about was Luke and how close he was. If he turned his head the slightest bit...if she turned hers...

His fingertips touched her cheek, and she turned her face towards the contact. Her heart stuttered when she discovered him watching her, unsmiling, his blue eyes fathomless in the dark of the evening, reflecting the bursts of fireworks but focused solely on her. Her mouth went dry, afraid he was going to kiss her and wanting him to so badly she thought she might die from it.

"Em."

In the din of the explosions she didn't hear him say her name but saw it on his lips. Locking her gaze with his, she let herself lean more into his shoulder, the only invitation she dared permit herself. It was all he needed. His gaze burned into her for one last second before dropping to her mouth. His fingers slid slowly over her chin to cup her jaw, cradling the curve in the palm of his hand. And finally, when she thought she would surely burst into flames, he kissed her.

His lips were warm and mobile, skilled and devastating. As Emily clung to his arm with her hand, she realized that there was never anything tentative with Luke. He was always strong, always sure of himself, and it took her breath away. He was always in control, and she wondered, quite dazzled, what it would take to make him lose that control? To lose it with her?

The finale began with rapid bursts of color crashing into the air. Emily's fingers dug into the skin of his arm, and she felt the vibrations of a moan in his throat as the kiss intensified, making everything in her taut with excitement and desire.

A final bang and gasp and then there was nothing but applause from the crowd.

Luke gentled the kiss, tugging at her bottom lip with his teeth before moving away, making her whole body ache with longing. His gaze was still on her, but there was something different in it now. Heat. And, Emily thought, confusion.

She looked past him to the crowd and was mortified to see Liz, Cait and their husbands watching. Liz's mouth had dropped open and Cait's soft eyes were dark with concern. Joe and Paul simply had goofy smiles on their faces. Emily looked past them, afraid that Sam had seen the sparks going off behind him rather than above, but he and the girls were still chattering excitedly about which bursts had been their favorites and the horrendous noise.

She scrambled to her feet and straightened her blouse. Luke took his time, getting to his feet and gathering the corner of the blanket to fold it. Emily grabbed the other side to help. She had to keep her hands busy. Avoid the assessing looks from Luke's family. Why had she let herself be carried away?

But she'd created another problem. Holding her side of the blanket meant folding it into the middle, which meant meeting Luke face-to-face. There was the silent question as which of them would take the woolen fabric to fold again. Emily dropped it, letting Luke fold it into a square.

Cait and Joe took the stroller and said goodbye, but Liz— bless her—acted as if nothing had happened and stopped to ask if Sam was going to day camp in the morning. Emily, Luke and Sam followed along back to the parking lot. Sam's feet started to drag, so Luke lifted him effortlessly on his shoulders and carried him to the truck.

Sam fell asleep on the drive home.

Emily couldn't bring herself to say anything to Luke. She didn't want to ask why. She didn't want to analyze it. She was terrified to ask what it meant or if it would happen again. The radio played a quiet country-and-Western tune and she stared out the window at the inky sky and the long, flat fields shadowed by the moon. When they reached the house, Emily was first to hop out and she took Sam in her arms.

"I need to get him into bed," she whispered, unable to meet Luke's gaze. He didn't protest or stop her. They both knew she was running away from what had happened. Her arms ached under Sam's weight—when had he grown so much?—and she was out of breath by the time she got to the top of the stairs. When she finally had him tucked between the sheets, she paused. The light was on in the kitchen. Luke was waiting for her, she knew it. She hesitated, her hand on the smooth banister. If she went down, they'd have to talk, and she was afraid to talk. She was afraid of spoiling the balance they'd achieved so effortlessly during the past week. She was afraid they'd stop talking, that he'd kiss her again. And she was afraid it would go further. Much further. She imagined him carrying her to his room, imagined feeling his skin against hers….

No, it was too much. So much more than she was prepared to give. To accept.

So she went into her own room and shut the door, biting her lip as she changed into her nightgown and slid between the soft cotton sheets.

Several minutes later she heard him turn off the light as he stopped waiting. His slow steps echoed on the stairs, creaking on the tread third from the top. The steps paused beside her door as her heart pounded with fear and, Lord help her, anticipation.

Then the steps went away and she heard him go into his room. Muffled sounds as he shed his clothing—she swallowed—and the sound of the mattress settling as he got in bed, his head only inches from hers, and yet so far away.

She lay awake for a long time, replaying the kiss, listening for his footsteps, and wondering what it was she wanted—if she even knew anymore.

The morning sun was high when Luke stopped to survey the herd below. Caribou's chestnut hide gleamed in the summer sun and the gelding tossed his head, anxious to get going again. Luke had taken the morning to check fence lines of the north pasture now that he and the hands had moved the herd east to graze on fresh grass. He could have done it on the quad, but he was a horse man at heart. Spending a morning in the saddle had sounded perfect at 7:00 a.m. when the dew was still heavy on the grass.

It had given him ample time to think.

Caribou shifted restlessly and Luke let him go, moving into a trot to the dirt lane that ran between sections. What the horse needed was a good run, a chance to burn off some energy. Luke could use it, too. He was wound tighter than a spring, and it was all due to Emily. Emily with her shiny mink hair and big eyes. Emily with her soft smiles and even softer skin. His fingers tightened on the reins. He'd been a damned fool last night, kissing her at the fireworks. It was bad enough it was in public, but with his family there? It was as good as putting a stamp on her as far as they were concerned.

And that wasn't his intention. Not at all. His sisters would pester him to death wondering what was going on. If Emily was "the one". It didn't matter that he'd made it clear there would never be a Mrs. Luke Evans. It was just better that way. He never wanted to saddle a wife with an invalid.

A yellow-headed blackbird bobbed in the bushes as he passed. What had been his intention, then? Why hadn't he just left Emily alone and kept his lips to himself? He'd asked himself that question all morning and had yet to come up with an answer. What did he want from Emily? Things had not changed. It would be pointless to start anything up knowing it could go nowhere.

He was right back to where he'd started—a fool. A fool to get so wrapped up in her that he'd given in to his wants and kissed her without thinking of the repercussions. Now she wasn't even talking to him. She'd scooted up to bed last night and had avoided him this morning with the excuse of getting Sam ready for day camp. All-business Emily. She'd made her feelings perfectly clear. It was better this way, but it made him snarly just the same.

The gate was up ahead. He slowed Caribou to a walk and squinted. Emily was coming through the gap, all long, tanned legs in beige shorts and a red T-shirt. His body gave a little kick seeing her waiting for him. Her hair glinted with surprising red tints but he couldn't see her eyes behind her sunglasses. He didn't need to. He could see by the tense set of her shoulders and the line of her lips that something was wrong.

He gave the horse a nudge and cantered to the gate where she was waiting, pulling up in a cloud of dust. It had to be important if she'd come all the way out here to find him.

"What is it? What's happened?"

She looked up at him and took off her glasses.

His stomach did a slow turn. The chocolate depths of her eyes were more worried than he'd seen them. "Is it Sam?"

His question seemed to break through and she shook her head. "No, no it's not Sam. He's still at day camp with the twins." She peered up at him, hesitated, then said gently, "It's your father, Luke."

His father. All his energy seemed to sink to his feet, making them heavy but the rest of him oddly numb. "Is he gone?" His voice sounded flat and he had the strange thought that for just a few moments the birds had stopped singing in the underbrush.

"No. But Liz called and they want you to come."

Relief struck, automatically followed by dread. He had known something like this was coming and had buried himself in work to avoid thinking about it. Dad was getting frailer by the day, and it had been nearly ten years since he had gone into the home—a long time for someone with his disease. Luke knew the facts. But it didn't make it any easier.

"Okay."

"Luke?"

He stared down at her. She was biting her lip and he watched as the plump pink flesh changed shape as her teeth worried the surface.

"You don't look so good, Luke."

He didn't feel so great either.

"What can I do to help you?"

He realized that she'd walked all the way out from the house in the July heat to find him. He held out a hand. "Get on. We'll double up going back to the house."

"But I...I can't get up there."

"Sure you can. I'll take my foot out of the stirrup. Give me your hand and swing up."

A brief look of consternation overtook her face and he felt his annoyance grow. Was she so turned off by his presence that she couldn't stand to touch him now? He held out his hand. "Come on, Emily. It's the fastest way back to the house. I need to get to town."

She put her foot in the stirrup and clasped his forearm,

taking a bounce and swinging her leg over the saddle so that she was shoehorned in behind him. The stirrups were too long for her now and Luke slid the toes of his boots back through as he slid an inch forward, giving her more room. Even so, they were spooned together and he felt every shift of her body torturing him as Caribou started off at a walk.

He swallowed tightly. It had to be bad if Liz had phoned in the middle of the day.

"Where's Sam?" It didn't escape his notice that Sam was absent.

"Day camp, remember?"

He hadn't remembered, and he felt a spark of panic before telling himself to exhale and relax. It had only been a momentary thing and he was distracted. He swiveled in the saddle, half turning to meet her gaze. "Right. You would never have left him alone. I know that."

He faced front again, frowning. Emily might know about his father but she hadn't put the other pieces together. The lists, the precise order. It was all there for a reason. Just because he'd forgotten about day camp didn't mean anything except he had other things on his mind.

And yet there was always that little bit of doubt.

Her hand rested lightly on his ribs, an additional point of connection. What would it feel like for her to put her arms around him and hold him close? He wished he could know, but it was better if he didn't. He knew she still didn't understand what it all meant—to his father, to this ranch, to him. And he didn't want to explain. Right now he just needed to get to the nursing home. To see his father, the shell of a man he remembered. To hope that it was not too late.

And maybe, just maybe…there was always the forlorn hope that his dad might even recognize him one more time.

"Hang on," he said. And when her arms snaked around his middle, holding on, he felt his heart surge as he spurred the gelding into a canter and hastened their way home.

CHAPTER TEN

EMILY WRAPPED HER arms around Luke's waist, feeling the steel waves of pain and resentment binding him up in one unreachable package. His strong thighs formed a frame for hers as they headed for the farmyard and barns. She wished she could be out riding with him under different circumstances. A pleasure ride, stopping beneath the shade of a poplar or walking along the irrigation canal. She wanted the Luke of last night back, even as much as that man frightened her with the force of her feelings. The man she clung to now was in pain. She knew how that felt, and she wished she could take it away, make it better for him somehow.

He slowed the horse to a walk when the barn was in view, letting Caribou cool down. Emily said nothing as she dismounted and then he hopped down beside her. Silently they worked, removing bridle and saddle and Emily slid the blanket from the gelding's back and draped it over a rail in the tack room. He turned Caribou out into the corral and locked the gate, still saying absolutely nothing. Emily was beginning to worry. She didn't want him going to town alone. When he was about to head for the truck, she stopped him with a hand on his arm.

"Wait. We'll take my car."

"I don't want you to go."

The clipped words were not unexpected, but they stung just

the same. He had not let her in since she'd arrived at the gate so now was no different. She knew that. She also knew he needed help. Whether he realized it or not, he'd been there for her when she needed it most. She would return the favor.

"Liz is there and someone will have to pick up the kids at day camp. And you're in no shape to drive. So shut up and this once let someone do something for you."

She stood her ground, staring him down and watched him struggle. Didn't he think she could see how he always took care of everyone else? She wasn't blind. Married or not, his sisters still turned to him when they needed him. And he was there. Seeing his face when she'd told him about his dad had been all she needed. Someone had to be there for Luke.

"We're only wasting time," she said, quieter now, but no less sure of herself.

"We'll take your car but I'm driving." He gave in with a terse nod.

She could agree to that, so long as he wasn't alone. "Give me two seconds to grab my purse and keys," she replied, already dashing to the house. Liz had sounded tearful on the phone. Emily didn't want to think the worst, but she was sure that that was what Luke was thinking and getting him there as soon as possible would be best for everyone.

Liz and Cait were waiting outside the nursing home, sitting on a bench surrounded by petunias and geraniums. Baby Janna was asleep, bundled in a carrier and Liz's youngest was in a stroller, playing with a bar of brightly colored toys hooked along the top. When Luke strode up the walk, Liz rose and went to him, wrapping her arms around his neck. Cait was slower getting to her feet but when she went to Luke, he opened an arm and she slid in beneath it.

Emily blinked back tears for the trio who bonded amid so much pain. In the absence of parents, Luke had been their father figure even if he'd only been a few years older. Seeing them through to adulthood must have been so difficult, but he had done what needed to be done. Emily hung back, watching Luke give his sisters a squeeze and then asking the difficult question: "How bad?"

Liz was sniffling and Cait had to answer. "He fell last night. Nothing is broken, but the doctor says…"

Luke waited.

"He says it's time for palliative care, Luke."

Pain slashed across Luke's face, but he stood strong. "We knew this day would come, Cait."

"It doesn't make it easier."

"I know it. I want to talk to the doctor."

Emily felt so very in the way. Luke didn't need her. He had his sisters. This was a family problem and she wasn't family. Still, there had to be something she could do to help. They all needed to be with their father. She stepped up and searched Luke's eyes, then Liz's.

"I'm so sorry about your father. Is there anything I can do?"

Luke shook his head. "Thank you for asking, Emily." He seemed to think for a minute, and then leaned over and dropped a kiss on her cheek. "You've already helped so much."

Emily's cheek burned where his lips had touched it, even if it had been an impersonal peck. She had a sudden idea and turned to Liz. "Why don't you let me pick up the twins? Then you can stay as long as you need."

Liz's face relaxed and Emily felt Luke's hand at her back, a gentle contact that told her she'd said the right thing.

"If you do, take them back to my house. Paul's gone to Medicine Hat but he'll be back later to take over. It would be a godsend, Emily."

"You need to be with your father, Liz. You all do. I can

take Alyssa, too. It's no trouble. You just do what needs to be done."

Liz gave her the house key and got the car seat out of her car while Luke wrote directions to Liz's house on a slip of paper. When the baby was installed in the seat and buckled safely in, Luke stayed behind.

"Em, I don't know how to thank you." He braced a hand along the window of the open door of her car.

"It's not necessary, Luke. I'm happy to do it. Otherwise I'd just feel helpless."

"Helpless?"

How could she explain that Luke—and his family—had come to mean so much to her? That seeing him hurting caused her to have pain as well? They'd known each other such a short time. Her mother had always said she had a heart as big as all outdoors. It kept getting her into trouble. She felt things too deeply.

"You know, sitting around, waiting for news. At least this way I feel useful." She looked up, discovered he was watching her with a curious expression and dropped her lashes again before she gave away too much. "You should go. See your dad and talk to the doctor. I'll catch up with you later."

"You're right," he replied, shutting the car door as she buckled her seatbelt.

She drove away, only looking in the rearview mirror once and saw Luke going through the doors with his sisters. She was glad she could help, but she would rather be with him, sitting by his side.

But he didn't want that or else he would have asked. He hadn't even wanted her to come along. As she turned down a quiet street, she blinked a few extra times to clear the stinging. She was glad now that she hadn't gone downstairs last night.

She was falling in love with Luke Evans, and hearing him say he'd made a mistake would be more than she could take.

Paul and Liz returned just after seven-thirty. Emily had fed the kids and the twins were curled up with Sam on the sofa watching a movie—the girls in pink pajamas and Sam in the spare sweats and T-shirt that he'd carried in his backpack to camp. Alyssa was sweet-smelling from her bath and Emily nuzzled the baby's neck lightly, inhaling the scent of baby lotion as she prepared an evening bottle. Caring for four had been busy, but fun. The laughter, the pandemonium—they were things that had been missing from Emily's house, having had an only child. She had reconciled herself to knowing that the large family she'd wanted would never happen. Now she wondered if she might find a second chance someday. She had to get her life in order first, but she realized her heart was not as closed to the idea as it had once been. After her divorce, she'd been so determined never to go down that road again. Never to put Sam in the position of getting hurt. And yet here she was. And for a moment she wondered if rekindling those dreams meant she was putting her own wants ahead of the needs of her son. How did that make her any different from Rob, who had chosen his own dream ahead of his wife and son?

As she sat in a rocker and fed Alyssa, she banished the uncomfortable idea and turned her thoughts back to Luke. She couldn't stop wondering about his father and what the doctor said. How was Luke holding up? She lifted the baby to her shoulder and began rubbing her back just as Liz and Paul drove into the yard. Em's heart did a little rollover as they came in the back door. Liz looked so weary, even as she greeted Emily and smiled.

"Thank you, Emily, for watching the kids. It means so much that I could stay with Cait and Luke and Dad today."

Emily's lips curved wistfully when Alyssa put her chubby arms out for her mother and Paul went into the living room to check on the older kids. She missed the feeling of the baby's weight on her arm, and her heart warmed when Alyssa tucked her head against her mother's neck, utterly contented as she stuck two fingers in her mouth.

"It was no trouble. The kids had fun, I think. I just made spaghetti for supper. There are leftovers in the fridge for you and Paul if you're hungry. I wasn't sure if you'd have a chance to eat."

Liz's eyes filled with tears as her fingers stroked the baby's hair. "Oh, Emily, you really are wonderful. I hope you don't mind me saying... Cait and I both hope you're here to stay more permanently."

Emily's heart ached. Staying meant staying with Luke and despite last night's kiss she knew it was impossible. "My plans are still the same, Liz. But I'll be here until the end of the summer. Hopefully things will have normalized with your father by then."

"That's not what I meant," Liz said, settling Alyssa on her arm. "After last night..."

"Don't read too much into it," Emily replied lightly, though butterflies went through her stomach as the memory danced through her mind. "It was just a kiss." A kiss that hadn't been mentioned again. It was almost as if it had never happened. As if neither of the kisses had happened now that Emily thought of it. And yet, at the time they had been heart-stoppingly intimate... The way Luke looked at her, as though she was the only woman on earth. The way his fingers touched her face. She hadn't imagined the connection between them. But they had just been caught in the moment. They had to be, for him to become so distant afterwards.

"I don't think it was just a kiss."

Emily needed to change the subject and while Liz and her

husband were back home—together—Emily wondered about Luke. "Is Luke still at the home?" she asked, busying herself with putting the children's dirty glasses in the dishwasher.

"Yes, he wanted to stay with Dad."

Alone. Emily felt annoyance niggle at her. Didn't his sisters realize that Luke needed support, too? Someone should be with him. Liz and Cait didn't have to go through this alone—why should Luke?

He needed her. She wished she were stronger. She wished she could stay emotionally uninvolved. That was her problem—she let herself feel too deeply. Her heart twisted as she realized he'd supported her at a time she needed it most. She couldn't turn her back on him. But there was Sam to think of, too. She wasn't sure the care home was the place for him, not at such a time. "I'll go pick him up," Emily said, reaching for her purse. "Can I come back and pick up Sam later?"

The sound of laughter at a song in the movie echoed from the living room. Liz's keen eyes watched her closely, but for once Emily didn't care what she thought. "Why don't you let him stay here? He can have a sleepover with the girls. We've got an air mattress and sleeping bag and it'll be fun. After what you did for me today—it's the least we can do. He can go to camp with the girls in the morning and you can pick him up after."

It was a perfect solution. "If you're sure…"

"Of course I'm sure. Don't be silly."

Emily settled everything with Sam, who was overjoyed and not the least bit apprehensive about spending the night away from her.

The evening had mellowed, losing the July glare and settling into a hazy, rosy sunset as Emily drove back to the nursing home. Inside, all was quiet. Her shoes made soft sounds on the polished floor. Dialogue from a television turned low murmured from a common room and the hushed voices of staff kept the place from feeling totally empty. She got the room number from an attendant and walked down a quiet hall. When she got to the correct room on the right she peeked around the doorway.

Luke was sitting in a chair beside the hospital bed, leaning forward with his elbows on his knees, the very picture of defeat. The blinds were closed and the only light came from a tiny lamp in the corner. There was no movement from the man beneath the white-and-blue sheets, but Emily could see that Luke had his father's hand folded within his own. There were tears on Luke's face; silent ones, leaving a broken, shining trail down his tanned cheeks, and he lifted his father's hand to his lips and kissed it.

Emily backed out of the room and leaned back against the wall, pulling in a shaking breath as she struggled to hold on to her composure. Luke was the strong one. Luke didn't show emotion. The man who handled everything without complaint was *crying*.

She closed her eyes. Everything slid into place, but it wasn't a comfortable feeling. She had fallen in love. It was unexpected and unwanted, but it was undeniable. She had been attracted to him from the beginning—to his strength, to his kindness, to his generosity. But it was this human side of him, the part that crumbled apart with his father's hand in his, that toppled her over the edge. Perhaps it was the sense that he had so much love to give but spent his life alone. Or perhaps it was sensing that he needed love so desperately. That he was hungry for it and would rather starve than ask for it.

Where it would lead she had no idea, nor was tonight the time to worry about it. Tonight, other things were more important. Like the fact that Luke was alone in there. His sisters had gone home to their husbands and families, but Luke had stayed. Who was there for him? To whom could he unburden himself at the end of the day? She'd told Liz the plan was the same—that she would be leaving at the end of the summer. It was still true. Luke did not return her feelings. She wouldn't delude herself into pretending he did, or wish for what wouldn't be. A few kisses meant little in the bigger scheme of things.

She hadn't meant to fall for him, and no one could be more surprised, but she'd spent enough time lying to herself in the past few years that she knew she had to be brutally honest. The timing was horrible—her whole situation was in flux and she was coming out of a devastating divorce. But she loved him. She would not be leaving the ranch with her heart intact. There was nothing she could do about it. It was too late.

Now she had two choices. She could back away, protect herself. Leave, if it came to that. Or she could take what precious time she had to help him through this.

There really was no contest. She was tired of running away from her failures and away from memories. This time she would stand.

"You always were a sucker for punishment," she murmured to herself. She let out her breath and stepped back around the corner.

Luke held his father's hand in his. It felt small now, and he thought of being a child and putting his hand within his father's wide palm, innocent and trusting. He'd worshipped his father, wanted to do everything just like him. He'd followed him through the barns and fields, learned to ride, learned to herd cattle and work the land. As he'd grown, they'd had their differences. New things had become important.

Luke had felt the need to stretch his legs, explore new places and people as he'd become a young man. They'd argued. There'd been resentment on both sides, but none of it mattered now. The tables were perfectly turned. Luke was the parent. His father was the one with the small hand, the one relying on Luke to be strong and do the right thing for everyone.

Only there was nothing he could do. There never had been, and knowing he was helpless was almost more than he could bear. Luke pressed the frail hand to his lips and felt the tears sting behind his eyes. He let them come, sitting in the semi-darkness, away from the forlorn gazes of his sisters and the sympathetic pats from the nurses. He let grief and exhaustion have its way for once. There was no one to see. No one to witness the coming apart that had been building since that horrible night when the fire department had come and he couldn't ignore the signs any longer. No one should have to go through this…this awful watching and waiting. He would never put anyone through such an ordeal. Never.

He'd made the promise long ago, but it had come with a price. Tonight he paid that price as he sat alone, wondering why the hell it had all gone wrong and wishing, with a sinking sense of guilt, that he could turn back the clock and do things differently.

He squeezed the hand and there was no squeeze back. Luke laid his head on the edge of the bed and wept.

The fingers on his shoulder were firm and strong and he knew in an instant it was Emily. Damn her for coming and seeing him like this. He swallowed against the giant lump in his throat, choking on the futility and pain as he struggled to regain control. He swiped his hand over his face, wiping away the moisture he'd allowed himself to indulge in. But she'd seen him this way. Broken. He hated that she could see his weakness, but it came as a relief, too. It felt good to stop pretending. He didn't have to be strong for her the way he'd always had to be for Cait and Liz. With Emily he could just be Luke.

Emily stood behind him and looped her arms around his neck, pressing her lips to the top of his head in a gentle kiss.

They stayed that way for a few minutes until he regained his composure, and then he reached for her hand, tugging her to his side and pulling an empty chair over alongside his.

"You came." His voice came out rough, and he cleared this throat quietly.

"Of course I did."

"I couldn't bring myself to leave him here alone. Not yet."

Emily held his hand in hers and her thumb moved over the top of his hand, warm and reassuring. "It's okay, Luke. It's all okay."

"I've never lost it like that before."

"Then it's about time. Would you rather be alone?"

She felt as if she was holding her breath as she waited for him to answer. He could send her away right now and that would be the end of it. It would break this damnable connection that seemed to run between them. It would solve his problems where she was concerned. He was going to have to send her away some time—they had no future together. Now was probably a good time. Before things went any further.

But he gripped her fingers, needing her. Wanting her to stay with him. "No. Stay, please."

She squeezed his fingers back, saying nothing. She just sat with him. Beside him, somehow knowing exactly what he needed. Just as she'd done all day. She'd come with him to the nursing home and she'd stepped in to help instinctively, making it easier on all of them. Helping him by helping his family. Emily was weaving herself into his life without even trying. God, even now he couldn't imagine going back to the empty house without her. He'd told himself that anything more was simple physical attraction. But he'd been wrong. He was falling for her. He cared about her. And he needed her. Perhaps that was the most disturbing of all. He didn't want to need anyone.

He knew in his heart he shouldn't be letting her get this close, but tonight he didn't have the strength to push her away. He looked down at his father's still features and felt his insides quiver.

Tonight he realized that people did not have to die for you to grieve for them.

Emily had no words to make things better, so she simply sat and held his hand. After nearly an hour, and when the shadows grew long, he finally sighed and lifted his head. "I think it's time to go." He looked around suddenly. "I never even thought—Emily, where is Sam?"

Emily smiled. It was the second time today he'd asked about her son—what a change from his attitude when she'd first arrived. "It's okay. He's staying at Liz's for the night. He was very pleased to be having a sleepover. When I left them, the kids were watching a Disney movie and eating popcorn."

"You left him with my sister?"

"Shouldn't I have?" She wondered why Luke was frowning at her.

"It's just...you don't let him out of your sight. You're the mama bear."

He was right. She was protective of Sam. "You were the one who said I had to stop holding on so tight. And tonight you needed me more."

His gaze clung to hers as the softly spoken words hovered in the room. She knew he would never admit needing her, but it was true. Sam was fine. Emily knew Luke had been right all along. She'd focused solely on Sam because he was all she had. That wasn't true any longer, but would Luke let her in?

"He's such a good boy, Emily."

She picked up her purse, her throat thickening as she recalled hearing Sam's laughter mingled with Luke's as he'd ridden around the corral. "I know."

"And you're a good parent. You always put him first."

Emily looked up at him as they shut off the light. She wasn't sure he was so right about that part. Lately she'd been putting herself and her own wants ahead of those of her son. She'd bought into Luke's logic that Sam was already going to miss the farm so why not let him enjoy it? But it was really her. She didn't want to leave yet. And as much as she wanted to be there for Luke tonight, that fact niggled at her.

"So are you, Luke. You looked after your sisters. You still do. It was so clear when you saw them today. They lean on you. You are their guidepost."

He shut the door quietly behind them and held her hand as they walked down the hall. "Not many understand that. But you do."

"I hope the girls realize it, too," Emily remarked. "I think they are so used to you being their rock that they forget you're human, too."

He stopped, staring at her with surprise. "What are you saying, Emily?"

She lifted her chin and looked right in his eyes, still red-rimmed from his visit with his father. "I mean they are so used to you looking out for them that they might forget you need support, too. It goes both ways."

"They were younger than me. They didn't see things the same way I did."

Emily nodded. "Undoubtedly. Is that why you've never married? You were too busy bringing up your sisters? Too busy living up to your responsibilities to have a relationship?" She squeezed his fingers. "How much have you really sacrificed, Luke?"

His jaw tightened. "I suppose I've never met the right one."

He tried to brush off her questions, but the tense tone of his voice made the attempt fall flat. What wasn't he saying?

She might take offense if the situation were different, but they both knew she was not a girlfriend. She wasn't sure what she was to him anymore. Not yet a lover, not just an employee, more than a friend.

They exited into the warm night, into fresh air and the scent of the roses that flanked the walkway. "It's more than that, isn't it?"

He let go of her hand. "What do you mean?"

Emily paused, letting Luke carry on for a few steps until he turned as if he was wondering why she wasn't keeping up with him anymore.

"I mean, you keep people at arm's length. Oh, now and again something comes through—like seeing you with your sisters, or when you held Sam during the storm, or tonight, with your father. But the rest of the time..." She paused, searching for the right words. "You're a fortress. And you're the gatekeeper, too. You decide who is allowed in, and you only show bits of yourself when you want."

He stared at her as if she'd slapped him.

"You don't know anything about it."

"Because you haven't told me."

He scoffed, turning away. "Like you've told me everything?"

What more was there to tell? She shrugged her shoulders. "I told you that Rob left us. I told you why and what's happened since. What more do you want? Because if I tell you that his leaving destroyed my confidence, made me question every single thing about myself, whether I was a good wife or mother, what are you going to do, Luke?" His face paled and he took a step backwards. She kept her voice calm, rational. "That's it exactly. You're going to close yourself off and run away. Because you don't let anyone get close. Even when they really, really want to be."

She wanted to reach him desperately. He was right, she hadn't told him everything, but she also hadn't felt she needed to. He seemed to understand anyway, and now she'd gotten defensive and attacked him on a night when he was already dealing with so much. "Please," she whispered, and heard her voice catch. "I don't want to argue. I want to help. Please let me in."

"I can't," he murmured, turning away.

"Is it really that bad?"

"Please, Emily." He begged her now. "Can we not do this right now?" His voice cracked on the last word. "That small, frail man in there is the last parental connection I have. He doesn't even recognize me. Do you know what I could give for one more moment of clarity, one more real conversation? To have him look at me and say my name? His organs are shutting down. My father is going to die. Maybe not tonight. Or tomorrow, or next week. But soon."

He put his hand on the car-door handle and sent her a look so full of pain that it hit her like a slap. He opened the door and shot out a parting stab: "What does it say about me that I'm relieved?"

Emily had broken through. Luke had opened up. But now she only felt despair, knowing she'd only ended up causing him more pain.

CHAPTER ELEVEN

THE CAR RIDE home was interminable. Luke kept his hands on the wheel and his mouth shut. What had possessed him to say such a thing in the first place? As they turned on to the service road leading to the ranch, he sighed and thought back over the years to all the visits. All the times that his father had been lucid; Luke and the girls had been hungry for those moments when they had their father again.

Then the more frequent times when his father had been forgetful, repeating himself, focused on one tiny detail about something that happened before Luke had ever been born. Or the times Dad got so frustrated that he lashed out, mostly with hurtful words but sometimes with hands. When that happened, Luke knew that his father would never be the same. He was an angry, hostile stranger. Yet, each time Luke visited there was a tiny bit of hope that it would be a good day. The death of those hopes took their toll on a man. All the things he'd said to Em he'd never breathed to another soul. It was her. She got to him with her gentle ways and yes, even with her strength. She had no idea how strong she was.

And she had no idea how much he loved her for it. Nor would she, ever.

Luke parked the car and got out. He got as far as the steps and stopped. He couldn't go in there. Not tonight.

"Are you hungry? Did you even eat since breakfast?"

Emily's voice was quiet at his shoulder but he shook his head. He wasn't hungry. He was just...numb. He wanted to grab on to her and hold on and knew he couldn't. Not just for him, but for her. The way she turned those liquid eyes up at him damn near tore him apart. She'd kissed him back, making him want things he had decided he could never have. She made herself invaluable in a thousand different ways and each one scored his heart.

He shook his head but still couldn't make himself climb the steps.

"Luke?" The quaver in her voice registered and he turned to look at her. Her big eyes were luminous with tears...for him? The weight of carrying everyone's emotions suddenly got heavier.

"You're scaring me," she whispered.

He had to snap out of it.

"I'm sorry, Em. I just...can't go inside. I don't know why." But he did know. The memories were there. And the fears lived there, too. They lived in the clues he left himself as an early-warning system, in the shadowed corners where he told himself he could never let anyone get too close.

It had worked up until now. Until Emily.

"Then let's walk. It's a beautiful night and I don't need to stay close to the house for Sam. Let's just walk a while, okay?"

Relieved, he nodded. Walking was good. He pointed north, knowing exactly where he needed to be. Emily took his hand and he let her hold it. The link made him feel stronger. Grounded him in a world spinning out of control.

The evening was as mellow as he'd ever seen it this early in July. The wide-open sky swirled together in shades of pink, peach and lilac as the sun began to dip over the prairie. Even the green leaves on the shrubs and poplar trees seemed less brash in the evening light. The air was perfumed with fresh grass and timothy and the faintest hint of clover. Why had he ever considered leaving, as though this place wasn't enough? The ranch was in his blood. Something tightened inside him. So many things were in his blood and that was the whole problem.

He led Emily over the fields to the top of a knoll. He stopped and took a deep breath. From here they could see for miles. Evans's land went on for a huge portion of the view. This was his. His responsibility. His heritage.

His privilege.

"Oh, wow," Emily breathed, and he looked over at her. Lord, she was beautiful. He'd thought so from the first. Her hair had grown a little longer in the days she'd been here, the flirty tips of her short cut now softer around her face. She had held him together today, as much as he didn't want to admit it.

"I'm scared, Em."

Sympathy softened her face even more. "Oh, Luke. I'm sure that is hard to say."

He nodded. "It is. I don't have the luxury of being scared. I've known for a long time that this family is my responsibility, but there was always this little bit of 'not yet' as long as Dad was alive. It was easier to deny, I suppose. I'm starting to have to face the truth. It's all on me now. And I don't want to face it. I want to go back to being twenty and full of myself and with my life ahead of me. Not predetermined."

He shook his head. "I'm a selfish bastard. I've got everything I could ever want and I'm ungrateful."

"No you're not." She turned her back on the view and gripped his wrists. "I can only imagine how hard this is for you. He is your father."

"I never asked for this. We were still reeling from Mom's death and I think Dad must have had an idea that things weren't right. He and I went to the lawyer's one day and he changed his will and gave me power of attorney. He told me it was because one day the farm would be mine. I had no idea how soon...I think he knew what was coming and was preparing. He knew I would have to make the decisions when he couldn't. But putting your own father in a home..." His voice cracked. "It was hell on earth making that decision."

Remembering how ungrateful he'd been back then left a bitter taste in his mouth. "I wanted to finish school. To get away from Evans and Son like it was a foregone conclusion." He stared past Emily's shoulder at the blocks of color below: the dull green of the freshly hayed fields, the lush emerald of pasture, the golden fields of grain crops. "We had words about it."

"And he was already sick?"

"Yes." He turned his attention back to Emily, expecting to see revulsion on her face. Hell, he hated himself for ever having felt it and now saying it out loud was like admitting he was a self-absorbed kid. But her eyes were soft with understanding, and she took a step forward and wrapped her arms around his waist, resting her head on his chest.

He let his arms go around her, drawing strength from her.

"We thought he was just grieving for Mom and having difficulties. We made all sorts of excuses. It wasn't until the smoke alarms went off that we realized. The kitchen had some fire and smoke damage. That was all. But it could have been worse. He was a danger to all of us. The hardest thing I ever did was put my father in a home. Especially after the words I'd said to him. And the girls...they were dealing with teenage angst and emotions and missing our mother. I was barely more than a kid myself."

He paused, wondered how much of the truth to tell her and settled for half. "I never want to have that responsibility again. I've been son, brother, parent, breadwinner and sole operator of this ranch and that's enough for me. I raised my family and it was one hell of a painful experience. I don't want to raise another one."

She pulled away from his chest. Perhaps he hadn't shocked her before but he had now. Her face had gone white as she stared up at him. What would she say if he told her the rest?

But he couldn't bring himself to say it out loud. And what good would it do for her to know he wanted things that he could never have? It would only hurt them both further, because it was as plain as the nose on his face that she was developing feelings. That was his fault, and up to him to fix.

"I see."

He swallowed, hating the dull pain in her voice. "I thought you should know so you didn't get..." Oh, God, this was tearing him apart on top of everything else. He didn't want to hurt her. "So you didn't get your hopes up. About us."

"You mean after the kisses." She dropped her hands from his ribs as though his skin was suddenly burning her fingertips. It was what he wanted. He needed to push her away, so why did it have to hurt so much?

"I shouldn't have kissed you. Either time. I certainly didn't plan it. You're a desirable woman, Emily. Don't let that fool of an ex-husband let you think otherwise. But I'm not in the market for a wife and you should know that from the start."

She turned her back on him, staring over the naked fields now with her shoulders pulled up. He *had* hurt her. He'd only hurt her more if he kept on. The sky was a dusky shade of purple and he knew they had to be going back. Off to the east, the first howl of a coyote echoed, lonely and fierce.

Emily turned back to face him and he expected to have tears to contend with. But there were none. Her face was impassive, showing neither hurt nor pleasure. She merely lifted her eyebrows the slightest bit and replied, "Then it is a good thing that I'm not looking for a husband, either."

* * *

Emily held herself together all during the long, silent walk back to the house, all the while she called Liz to check up on Sam, and even up until she brushed her teeth and climbed under the covers of her bed. But once she put her head on the pillow, the tears came. She would not sob; she refused to let Luke know that she was crying over him. Hadn't it only been short weeks ago she'd claimed she'd hardened her heart to love? How wrong—how arrogant—she'd been. She'd had chinks in her armor and Luke had got past each one. She hadn't even recognized the feeling inside her as hope, but it had been there. She had envisioned getting on with her life. The possibility of more children, the big family she'd always longed for. Who was she kidding? She had pictured it happening with Luke. Maybe not right away. But somewhere in the back of her mind he'd emerged as her ideal.

She sniffled into her pillow, her heart hurting. Hadn't she just done the same thing as before? She had given of herself. Anyone could cook and clean, but it had been more than that. She'd done so with care, trying to make things better for Luke. It had been personal from the start. She'd been looking for his approval, she realized. Not approval of the job but approval of her. She'd set herself up for this. It wasn't all Luke's fault.

She was conscious of him lying in the next bedroom, and struggled to keep her breathing quiet. She couldn't stay here. She couldn't face him day after day, feeling the way she did, and knowing it would never go anywhere. Oh, she couldn't just pack up and leave in the morning. She would give it a few days. Let things resume some sort of normalcy, give Luke a chance to get his father settled. But it was time to go back to the old emergency plan. At least now she had an idea of what she could do. She was good at taking care of people and she loved children. She would go to her parents' place, find work as a housekeeper and look into some night courses. She could take early childhood education or perhaps even a teaching assistant course—both positions that would mean she could support Sam in all the ways that mattered.

She fluffed her pillow and let resolve flood into her. Thinking ahead felt so much better than the hurt. The idea took hold and she closed her eyes, desperate to look forward, willing sleep to come.

She had simply been lonely, thinking of herself, swept away by fancy. But she couldn't afford to think only of herself. She had Sam, and he came first. In time she'd stop caring about Luke Evans and simply thank him for showing her the way to her independence.

Sleep snuck in, merciful but bittersweet. If that were true, then why did she still feel this aching hole inside her?

CHAPTER TWELVE

JOHN EVANS WENT into the palliative care unit the following afternoon. Emily scrubbed bathrooms, brought clothes in off the line and picked Sam up from camp as Luke and his sisters spoke to the doctor and care worker. She did not offer to go with Luke and he didn't ask her. After his revelations of the night before, it seemed like an unspoken conclusion that he would handle things on his own. It felt as though they'd said all that could be said, and yet so much seemed left unspoken.

For three days Luke worked the farm, Emily fulfilled her housekeeping duties and Sam finished camp and played with Homer in the hot July evenings.

Each day tore into Emily's heart a little more. She saw Luke struggling with emotions, the wear and tear showing in the lines on his face and the weary set to his shoulders, though he never complained. He never talked to her about it either, not after that last night when he'd been so open and honest and sharing. It was, she realized, all she was going to get from him. Whatever had been between them—for his part—had run its course. It wasn't the same for her. Each bit of distance between them cut a little deeper. She was surer than ever that she had to go. It hurt too much to stay.

She waited until Sam was in bed one night before giving Luke her notice.

"Luke?"

He looked up from the magazine he was reading. A summer shower was falling and he'd turned on the lamp behind him, casting the room in a warm glow. It was so cozy here. So... right. But Luke didn't love her, and she couldn't survive staying without it. She wanted more. She needed more, deserved more...and so did Sam. If nothing else, Luke's turning her away had made her realize that she was the marrying kind. Even after the disaster of her first marriage, she still believed in it. Still believed in two people making that commitment to each other. She knew now that her words to the contrary had only been a way to cover up the pain of failing the first time.

And she was not the one who had given up. She wasn't the one who had walked away. No, it was all or nothing with her, even now. And she was asking more than Luke could give. No, it was time to cut her losses. Moving forward would be best for her and best for Sam.

"This isn't going to work. I know I should give you more notice, but..." she swallowed and gathered her strength, forcing out the next words. "Sam and I are going to leave tomorrow. We're going to my mom and dad's in Regina."

Luke's face showed nothing, until she looked into his eyes. Steely blue, they met her gaze, and there was surprise and perhaps regret. But whatever his feelings, he shuttered them away again as he folded the cover back over the magazine and put it down. "I was afraid you were going to say that."

For the briefest of moments, her heart surged, but the flare quickly died. He'd expected this. And there was nothing in either his words or his expression to tell her he was going to ask her to change her mind.

"Thank you for all you've done for us." Oh, how awful that sounded. She pushed forward. "Working for you made me see that I'm good at this. I was looking for an office job and overlooked the job I've been doing for years. What you said about school...I'm going to look into childhood education. I love children and I think I'd be good at it."

And if that meant surrounding herself with the children of others rather than her own, that was okay. She'd do the best she could and she would provide a good life for her son.

"You'll be wonderful at it, Emily." He offered her an encouraging smile. "You're a wonderful mother. Kind and patient and firm."

The words were the right ones, but the polite, friendly tone cut into her.

"Thank you." She lifted her chin. "I realized I was overlooking my skills rather than capitalizing on them."

His gaze settled on her warmly. "You've made such a difference here. Not just with what you do, but with your kindness and generosity."

Her breath seemed stuck in her chest. Really, this polite veneer was killing her. She wanted to demand that he fight for her. That he tell her he hadn't meant to slam the door on them so completely. Something to let her know that he cared, that they had a chance. But he said nothing. He was as determined as ever to keep her out.

"I need to finish packing. Excuse me, Luke."

"I'll write you a check for your wages."

How could she take money? It seemed to cheapen what they'd had. And yet what did they have, really? Some feelings and a few kisses. She had to take the money. Not just because she needed it, but because if she refused he would know. He'd know that this had gone way beyond a business arrangement and into deeply personal territory, and she'd been hurt and humiliated enough.

"Thank you, Luke."

He picked up his magazine again and Emily felt her tenuously held control shatter. Without saying another word, she left the room and went upstairs to pack her suitcase.

* * *

When her footsteps sounded on the stairs, Luke dropped the magazine and ran a rough hand over his face. Keeping up the pretense just now had damn near killed him. The last few days had been hell. Not just putting Dad in the palliative care unit, but wanting, needing Emily beside him and knowing he'd been the one to turn her away. What had he expected she'd do after his cold words? He'd thanked her and then flat-out told her they had no future. She'd answered him back in kind but he'd seen the hurt behind her eyes. He never should have hired her. Never should have kissed her. Definitely never should have fallen in love with her. She made him want things he couldn't have—the home and wife and marriage that seemed to make everything complete.

She didn't understand why he was turning her away, or that he was doing it for her own good. And she sure as hell didn't know what it was doing to him to let her go.

Marriage was enough of a risk, and Emily had already lost once. He couldn't ask her to take a gamble on him when she didn't even know the odds. And the odds had been all too clear as he watched his father slide further and further away. He could end up just like his father. Then where would Emily be? And Sam? Looking after an invalid? Making heart-breaking decisions they way he'd had to?

She didn't know what it was like. Couldn't know unless she'd been through it.

He'd heard her crying in her room. Quietly, but crying just the same, and it had taken every ounce of restraint not to go to her and tell her he didn't mean it. Her leaving came as no surprise, and he had tried his best to make it easier on her. He pushed out of the chair and went to the office, digging out the checkbook and taking a pen from the holder. His hand shook as he filled out her name and the date and the pen hovered over the amount.

How could he put a price on all she'd given to him?

In the end he figured out her wage and doubled it, then ripped it out of the book and put it in an envelope, licking and sealing the flap.

He'd check her car's oil and fluids before she left, too. He realized that he'd never made good on his promise to teach her how to do those things for herself. But he'd do them this time. Just to be sure she got to Regina okay.

And maybe one day she'd realize that letting her go was the kindest thing he could have done.

It was still raining the next morning when Emily put Sam's suitcase in the trunk. Sam wore a sullen look. "I don't want to leave the fun kids. I don't even know Grandma and Grandpa. They're old and I won't have anyone to play with. And I was teaching Homer to roll over!"

"Sam!" Emily felt her patience thin. "Your grandparents love you. And you will make new friends."

Sam got into the car without another word and Emily sighed, regretting the sharp tone. Inside her purse was the envelope Luke had given her with her pay inside. She couldn't bear to open it and see the last glorious weeks reduced to a number sign. Luke stood nearby, straight and uncompromising. But when Emily slammed the trunk shut Sam opened his door and scrambled out again, running to Luke and throwing his arms around Luke's legs.

Luke lifted him as if he weighed nothing and closed his eyes as Sam put his arms around his neck.

Emily couldn't watch. She wasn't the only one who had come to care for Luke. Sam idolized him, and would have followed him around as faithfully as Homer if Emily had allowed it. Luke had patiently taught Sam how to sit on a horse and the difference between garden plants, the taste of hay ready for cutting and how the cattle could tell a man when bad weather was imminent. He had so much to give and refused to give it.

"Bye, squirt. Be good for your mom, okay?"

"Okay, Luke. Bye."

Emily vowed not to cry, but it was a struggle. She finally met Luke's gaze and nearly crumpled at the pain in the blue depths. All he had to do was say the word and she'd stay. One word. The moment hung between them until she was sure she would break.

"Goodbye, Emily."

She hadn't truly realized what the term *stiff upper lip* meant until she forced herself to keep her own from trembling. She swallowed twice before she trusted herself to say the words, "Goodbye, Luke."

She turned to go to the driver's-side door but he spoke again. "I checked your oil and everything last night. You should be fine now."

Stop talking, she wanted to say. Didn't he know each word was like the lash of a whip? "Thank you," she murmured, her hand on the door handle.

"Emily…"

His hand closed over hers on the handle. She slowly turned and his arms cinched around her.

The light rain soaked into the cotton of his shirt, releasing the scent of his morning shower and fabric softener as he cradled her against his wide chest. She clung to him, her arms looping around his ribs, holding him close. Did this mean he'd changed his mind?

All too soon he let her go and opened her door. She stepped back, her lip quivering despite her determinations. She had to face the truth. Luke's resolve that he'd raised his family—that he didn't want the responsibility—was stronger than any feelings he had for her. Numbly she got into the car and dropped her purse on the passenger seat while Sam sat, silent, in the back.

"Be happy," Luke said, and shut her door.

She turned the key and the engine roared to life. She put it in gear and started down the driveway.

At the bottom she glanced in the rearview mirror. He was still standing in the same spot, his jeans and flannel shirt a contrast to the gray, dismal day. She snapped her gaze to the front and to the wipers that rhythmically swiped the rain from the windshield.

She had to stop looking back. From now on it was straight ahead.

Luke went back into the house once her car had disappeared from sight. He closed the door and the sound echoed through the hall. His footsteps seemed inordinately loud in the empty kitchen. He should go to the barn and tackle a few of the tasks he'd been saving for a rainy day. Instead he found himself wandering aimlessly from room to room, ending in the living room. A white square caught his eye and he went to the old stereo, picked up the piece of paper and stared at her elegant handwriting.

If he'd ever wondered if she could do everything, here was his answer. After all these years of the record player not working, she'd fixed it.

He carefully moved the picture frames from the top, stacking them to one side as he lifted the hinged cover. Memories hit him from all sides: being at his grandparents' house and hearing the old albums, then his mom and dad bringing it home and putting on the Beatles and Elvis. Those LPs were still there, but Luke flipped the switch and sent the turntable spinning, placing the needle on the album already in place.

The mellow voice of Jim Reeves singing "I Love You Because" filled the room. Oh, how he'd complained as a boy when his parents had put on the old-fashioned tunes. Now he was hit with a wave of nostalgia so strong it almost stole his breath.

And as he listened to the lyrics, he wished he could take back the words that had sent her away.

What was done was done. He'd stayed strong despite it all, loving her too much to sentence her to a life of pain and indecision. But damn, it hurt.

It hurt more than he'd ever imagined possible.

Sam held a bouquet of black-eyed Susans, daisies and corn-flowers in his hand as Emily cut more stems for the bouquet. Her mother's wildflower garden was a rainbow of blooms right now, and Emily snipped a few pinky-purple cosmos blossoms to add to the mix. Sam waited patiently, but as Emily handed over the last flowers, she knew. He wasn't happy. And she knew why. Nothing had been the same since they'd left Luke's.

"What's the matter, sweetheart?" She forced a cheerful smile. "Aren't the flowers pretty for Grandma?"

"I guess," he muttered, looking at his feet rather than the profusion of flowers in his hand. Emily sighed. One of them pouting was enough.

"Grandma made cookies today. Why don't we have some once these are in water?"

He shrugged. "They're not as good as yours."

Emily knelt beside him. "I know there have been a lot of changes lately. And I know it's been tough, Sam. But Grandma and Grandpa are very nice to let us stay with them."

More than nice. They'd welcomed Emily and Sam with open arms and without the criticism Emily had expected. She'd come to realize their lack of contact over the years had been partly her fault. She'd always seemed too busy to visit and hadn't been as welcoming as she should have been. It was good to mend those fences, but it wasn't enough. Sam wasn't the only one discontented. Emily compared everything to Luke's house. Not as modern or updated as her parents' home but with far more character and redolent with decades of happy memories. The garden here was pretty, but she found herself wondering if the peas and beans were ready and if Luke was finding time to pick them. The wheat was ripening in the fields and she pictured Luke with the Orrick boys, high on a tractor amid the waving golden heads. August was waning and Labor Day approaching, and she wondered if he'd celebrate with Liz and Cait and the children. Remembering Canada Day caused such a chasm of loneliness that she caught her breath.

She thought about his father, and if he was still hanging on or if the family was grieving.

She had thought it would take time to forget about him, but forgetting had proved an impossible endeavor.

"Mom?" Sam's voice interrupted her thoughts and she forced a smile.

"What, pumpkin?"

He scowled. "You aren't supposed to call me pumpkin anymore."

"What should I call you?" She smiled. Sam was her one bright spot. She'd begun working part-time for a local agency and he met her at the door every single time she came home. He brought her books every night, first learning to read his own and then settling in for a bedtime story. He would start school soon and she was determined to sign up for her courses and find them their own place. But there were some days, like today, when she missed when he'd been a toddler, and names like pumpkin had been okay. What would she do when he was older and didn't need her anymore?

"I don't know. No baby names."

"I'll try. No promises." She grinned and ruffled his hair.

"I miss Luke. And Homer. And the horses. And the kids."

Oh, honey. She missed all those things, too, and more. Mostly Luke. She wanted to promise Sam everything would be better soon, but it seemed unfair. He was entitled to his feelings. He shouldn't be made to feel as if they were insignificant.

"Me, too, sweet...Sam," she amended, gratified when he smiled. "But we knew all along that it was temporary, remember?"

"I thought...maybe..."

"Maybe what?"

"That Luke was going to be my new dad. When he kissed you and stuff."

She felt her cheeks color. "How do you know about that?"

He shrugged again—a new favorite five-year-old gesture since his birthday. "I saw you. At the fireworks. Everyone did."

Emily stood up and took his hand, starting towards the house. "Luke and I liked each other for a while," she said, not sure what to tell him that would explain things without getting complicated. "But it wasn't like that," she finished awkwardly.

"I wish it was. I liked it there. Even better than Calgary."

They'd reached the back steps when her cell phone vibrated in her pocket. "Go inside and give these to Grandma. Bet she'll give you an extra cookie." Emily took the phone out of her pocket and her heart took a leap as she saw Luke's name on the call display.

It vibrated in her palm, and before she could reconsider she flipped it open and answered it.

"Hello?"

"Emily?"

Oh, his voice sounded just as rough and sexy over the

phone. Her spine straightened and her fingers toyed with the hem of her top. He could still cause that nest of nerves simply from saying her name.

"Luke. Is everything okay?" She knew he'd never call unless something was wrong. He'd said all that he'd needed to say.

"Dad's gone, Emily."

His voice cracked at the end. There was a long pause while Emily wondered if he was going to continue. Her throat tightened painfully. "Are you okay, Luke?"

He cleared his throat. "I think so. I need to ask you a favor."

Anything. She almost said it, hating herself for being so easy even if it was only on the inside. Her fingers gripped the phone so tightly her knuckles cramped. "What is it?"

"Can you come?"

Her knees wobbled and she sat down on the back steps, the cool cement pricking into her bare legs. "You want me to come for the funeral?"

"Yes. And to talk."

Her breath caught in her chest. She hadn't thought she'd ever hear his voice again, let alone see him. But she couldn't get her hopes up. "Talk about what?"

"There were things I should have said but didn't."

"You seemed to say enough." He had been the one to turn her away, and now he expected her to come when he crooked his finger? She knew it was a difficult time for him and she wanted to help, but she refused to put herself in the position of being hurt again.

"I know, and I need to explain."

"I don't know…" She wanted to be there for him, but the wounds were still too fresh. She was still too close to be objective.

"The service is the day after tomorrow. If you can't get away, I'll come to you afterwards. Give me your address."

Come here? Impossible. As kind as her parents had been, Emily had glossed over her pain at leaving Alberta. She'd let them believe she was so down because of her divorce—they had no idea she'd been foolish enough to have her heart broken all over again. Luke showing up here would create all sorts of problems. Especially considering what Sam had just said.

"No, I'll come," she decided. If it was that crucial, she'd take a day and go.

"Thank you, Emily. It means a lot."

What was she doing? Setting herself up for another round of hurt? Getting over him was taking too long. Maybe they would be better this way. Despite what had happened, it felt as if they'd left loose ends. Maybe they needed to tie those off. Cauterize the wound so she could finally heal.

"I'm sorry about your dad," she said quietly, pressing the phone to her ear, not wanting the conversation to end so soon. Lord, she *had* missed him. The line went quiet again and she thought she heard him take a shaking breath. Her heart quaked. She had so many things she wanted to say, and her one regret over all these weeks was that she'd never told him exactly how she felt. Would it have made a difference if he'd known she was in love with him?

"We'll talk about it when you get here," he replied.

After the phone went dead, Emily sat on the steps a long time. She was going back. The memory of his face swam through her mind, scowling, smiling, and that intense, heart-stopping gaze he gave her just before he kissed her. She would see him the day after tomorrow.

If nothing else, she would tell him how she felt. How his dismissal of her had cut her to the bone. And then she would let him go once and for all.

CHAPTER THIRTEEN

EMILY TURNED UP THE drive at half past twelve. The midday sun scorched down and Emily noticed the petunias in the baskets were drooping, in need of a good deadheading and watering. Luke's truck sat in the drive, and the field equipment was lined up in a mournful row next to the barn. The farm work had ceased for today, a sad and respectful silence for the man who had started it all and passed it on to his son.

His son. Luke stepped through the screen door and on to the porch as she parked. He rested one hand on the railing post while Emily tried to calm both the excitement of seeing him again and the sadness of knowing the reason why he'd traded in his jeans and T-shirts for a suit. Black trousers fitted his long legs and the white shirt emphasized the leanness of his hips and the breadth of his shoulders. The gray tie was off-center and her lips curved up the tiniest bit. Luke was the kind of man who would hate being bundled up in a tie.

She stepped out of the car. Her shoes made little grinding noises on the gravel as she walked to the house. Luke waited as she put her shaking hand on the railing and climbed the steps to the porch.

God, how she'd missed him. She faced him, drinking in every detail of his features. Regular Luke was irresistible. But this dressed-up Luke felt different and exciting. He'd had a haircut recently—a razor-thin white line marked the path of his new hairline. His mouth, the crisply etched lips that remained unsmiling, and his eyes. She stopped at his eyes. She had expected pain and sadness. But what she saw there gave her heart a still-familiar kick. Heat. And desire.

"You look beautiful," he said quietly. He reached out and took a few strands of her hair in his fingers. "You let your hair grow."

She reached up and touched the dark strands without thinking. When she realized what she was doing she dropped her hand to her side again. "I felt like a change." She meant to speak clearly but it came out as a ragged whisper. If she reacted like this now, how would they make it through a whole afternoon?

"Emily…"

She waited. As the seconds passed, she wondered how long before they would have to leave for the church. He'd said he wanted to talk to her, but they wouldn't have much time. Surely he had to be there early. To be with his sisters. To say goodbye. With every second that slid past she felt Luke sliding away as well.

Luke drew in his eyebrows and pushed away from the post. Emily took a step forward and put her hand on his forearm. Her fingers clenched the fine white fabric and she got a little thrill as the muscle hardened beneath her touch.

"Why is it so hard to say what I need to say?" he wondered aloud, putting his hand over hers. "I've said it a million times in my head, Em. Over and over again since you left."

Emily looked up. In her heels she was only a few inches shorter than he was and impulsively she tipped up her face, touching her lips to his. "Then just tell me," she whispered, meeting his gaze evenly. "I came all this way…"

"Yes, you did." He smiled a little then. "You were always there when I needed you, Em. Right from the start. Until I sent you away. I kept looking for your car to drive up the lane because somehow you always seemed to know what I needed. But you didn't come."

"You made it all too clear in those last hours that I wasn't needed at all."

"It's completely my fault." He cupped her jaw with a wide hand. "I'm the one who forced you to leave."

"You didn't force me anywhere. I left because you made it clear you were not interested in pursuing anything further. And because my own feelings were already involved."

She could give him that much. She did want to tell him how she felt, but he was the one who had asked her here. He was the one who'd said he had something to tell her. Whatever it was, she wanted him to get it off his chest.

His gaze warmed as he looked down at her. "I know they were," he said quietly. "It was why I needed to stop what was happening between us before it went too far. I needed to push you away so I didn't have to face things. I didn't tell you everything, Em, that night on the hill. I held back the real reason why I promised never to let myself get too close to anyone. And I hurt you because I was too afraid to say it out loud. If I didn't say it, there was still part of me that could deny it."

"Then tell me now," she replied, gripping his hand, drawing it down to her side. "I'm here. I'm listening."

"It's more than I deserve."

"It's not. You gave me—us—so much while we were here." Emily took a deep breath, gathering her courage. "I fell in love with you, Luke."

The blue depths of his eyes got suddenly bright. "Don't say that, Em…"

"And as often as you looked for me to come back, I waited for the phone to ring. Hoping it would be you. I promised myself if I got another chance, I'd tell you how I felt. Because you need to understand. I vowed I would never love anyone again after what I'd been through. I swore I would never put

Sam through anything like that ever again. And I fell for you so hard, so fast, it was terrifying."

He pulled her close, his hands encircling her back and she closed her eyes. For weeks she'd despaired of ever feeling his arms around her again. Now she hung on as if she would never let go.

All too soon he pushed her away. "I can't," he said, running a hand over his closely cropped hair. "I can't do this. Please Em…let's sit."

She sat on the plush cushion of the porch swing, the springs creaking as he sat beside her and put his elbows on his knees. It had taken all she had to say the words and she was glad she had. For a brief, beautiful moment she had thought it was all going to be okay. But he kept pushing her away because of this…something that he still kept hidden inside. "I think you'd better just come out with it," she suggested. "Whatever it is, I can take it, Luke."

"Did you know there's a hereditary component to Dad's disease?"

Light began to glimmer as she realized what he was saying, and what he wasn't. Why hadn't she considered he'd be afraid he'd get it, too? "No. No, I didn't know that. It must be a worry for you."

Luke twisted his fingers around and around. "Sometimes early onset is completely random. But sometimes it's not. My father was fifty-three, Emily. At a time when my friends' fathers were going to graduations and giving away brides, my dad was forgetting who his children were, getting lost on roads he'd travelled most of his life. He should never have been around machinery or livestock—looking back, it's amazing something didn't go drastically wrong sooner. He could have killed us all that night if the smoke detectors hadn't been working. And I bore the brunt of it, don't you see? I resented it and felt guilty about it. Now he's gone, and it's a relief. Not because I wanted him to die, but because…"

His voice broke. "Because he was already gone and we simply spent the last years hoping for crumbs. That might be me down the road, and I won't do that to a family. I won't put them through what I went through. The pain and guilt and awful duty of caring for someone like that."

"Luke…"

"No, let me finish. I didn't turn you away because I didn't care about you. It's because I care too much to see you destroyed by having to go through what I went through."

She swallowed against the lump in her throat. He wasn't saying he didn't love her. He was putting her first, trying to keep her safe, and it made her want to weep. "Shouldn't that be my choice, Luke?"

"You don't know what you're asking." His voice was suddenly sharp and his eyes glittered at her. "Emily…" He put his head in his hands for a moment, taking a deep breath, collecting himself.

"How can you say no to something when you aren't even sure?" She felt him slipping away and fought to keep him there, in the moment with her. "There are no guarantees in this life, Luke. Are you willing to sacrifice your happiness for something that might or might not happen?" She paused. Put her hand on his knee and squeezed. "Are you willing to sacrifice *my* happiness, and Sam's? Because we both love you. We love you and we love this farm."

"Don't make it any harder than it has to be."

"Too late." She surprised herself with the strength of her voice. "It's already done. Look at me."

His gaze struck hers and she forged ahead. "You cannot keep me from loving you, Luke. I already do. Turning me away now won't prevent me from being hurt."

"I'm doing this for you!" Luke sprang off the seat and

went to the verandah railing, gripping it with his fingers. "I'm thirty years old. I might only have a few years left before symptoms...before..."

He turned his head away, unable to voice the possibilities.

He was terrified. Emily understood that now. He'd been through hell and he was making decisions based on that fear. She could understand that so well. Heck, she'd been there just a few months ago. So afraid of being hurt again that she was prepared to spend the rest of her life alone. But Luke had changed that for her. She went to him and touched his arm, pressing her cheek against his shoulder blade.

"You're afraid. I know you think that by sacrificing yourself you're keeping others from being hurt. I know what it is to be scared. When I left Calgary, I swore I would never fall in love again. That I would never make myself that vulnerable. The sudden loss of my marriage did a number on me. I blamed myself. I thought I wasn't good enough. And then I met you. You don't think I'm still scared?" She gave a little laugh. "You talked to me about dreams, but it isn't easy to follow dreams, especially when you have a five-year-old boy depending on you to keep his world safe and happy. I felt like every time I hoped for something more I was being self-indulgent. Not putting Sam first." She turned him around so he was facing her. "I was so scared to love you that I packed up and left. But I'm not leaving now, Luke. I'm sticking around. Nothing changed in my heart when I left except that you were here and I was there. I refuse to let you sacrifice your life for me."

"You don't know what it means," he repeated. "Dad was early onset. We were told long ago that there is a fifty-fifty chance that we kids have the genetic mutation."

Fifty-fifty. For a moment Emily quailed. It was difficult odds.

"And have you been tested?"

He shook his head, staring out over the lawn that was starting to brown in the late summer heat. "The girls did. Their risk is low. They married and had the children…"

A muscle ticked in his jaw. "How could I marry, knowing I might pass this on to my own children? To give them a life sentence like that?"

"Then why not be tested?"

He shook his head. "And what? What if I have the gene? I'd spend every day wondering how old I'd be when I started showing symptoms. I'd question every time I forgot the smallest detail, wondering if this was the beginning. I can't live that way, waiting for the other shoe to drop."

Tears gathered in Emily's eyes. Suddenly everything made sense. The absolute precision of the tools in the workshop, each piece hung on exactly the right peg. The list he kept on the fridge with the pay and work schedule. It had seemed obsessively organized at the time, but now she understood. It was his safeguard. An early-warning system, a way to keep him on track just in case.

He said knowing would make him question. But not knowing was doing the exact same thing.

"You already are," she whispered. "All the things in the house, just so. Numbers and to-do lists and having everything in a specific place…"

"I knew that if something was out of place, and I couldn't remember putting it there…"

Silence dropped like an anvil.

"You are already living the disease, Luke." The look of utter shock that blanked his face made her smile. She grabbed his hands and squeezed them. "Don't you understand? You are so afraid of dying that you stopped living. You're already second-guessing everything and missing out on what might be the happiest time of your life. Love, Luke. A wife and children. Laughter and happiness. You have given your family all of yourself. What is left for you?"

"I don't know."

"If there wasn't this disease hanging over your head, what would you do?"

"But there is…"

"Forget it for a minute. If you were free of it…"

Luke looked down into her glowing face and felt something he hadn't felt in over a decade—hope. He had been so afraid. Hell, he still was. But her question penetrated the wall he'd built around himself. If there was no chance of being ill? It was an easy answer.

"I'd ask you to marry me."

She hadn't expected that response, he realized, as her face paled and she dropped her hands from his arms.

He glanced at his watch, knowing he didn't have much time. Liz and Cait expected him to be there soon and this might be his only chance to say what he needed to say. He'd wanted to make her understand that his reasons went far deeper than not wanting responsibility. Her ex-husband had destroyed so much of her confidence. If he could only give her one thing, it was that he wanted her to know that this was about him. That she had so much to offer someone.

But she was making him want things he'd convinced himself he'd never have. More than want. It was so close he could see it all within his reach.

"It occurs to me that in less than an hour from now I'm going to bury my father. And if I continue the way I'm going, I'm going to bury myself right with him, aren't I?"

She nodded ever so slightly.

"You are the strongest woman I have ever met, Emily Northcott. No woman in her right mind would choose this. You should be running right now."

"But I'm not."

"No, you're not." His heart contracted as he realized the gift she'd truly given him. "You were strong for me when I wasn't strong enough for myself. And I love you. But it doesn't change the facts."

"Then take the test."

"As long as I don't, there's still hope…"

And as long as he didn't, it would hang like a noose around his neck, slowly tightening. They both knew it.

"If I took the test…if it came back positive…would you promise to leave me?"

When he looked down at her face there were tracks of tears marring her makeup. "No," she whispered. "I would not make such a promise. I would stay with you. No matter what the test says."

"I don't want this for you…"

"When you love someone you love all of them. Even the bits that aren't perfect." She smiled, though her lower lip quivered. "You know that, Luke. You knew it when you took in Homer. When you took in two lost strays like Sam and me."

"You should have more children," he continued, quite desperate now. "I know you want them. You said so when you talked about going back to school. I can't put this on another generation, Emily."

"Then you'd better have the test. Because you deserve to be a father, Luke. If not to your own…" she smiled up at him wistfully. "Sam adores you."

"You're asking me to make this permanent?"

"Yes. Yes I am. Either way. Unless you didn't mean it when you said you loved me…"

Luke gripped her shoulders. "I love you more than I thought I could ever love anyone!"

She smiled at him so sweetly he gathered her up in his arms and held on. "Damn, what did I ever do to deserve you?" His voice was ragged. Was it really possible? Could he possibly have a normal life? A wife and the son he'd always wanted? Sam was a gift. The son of his heart if not genetics. Over the last weeks, Luke had found himself listening for Sam's laugh and missing it terribly. It had seemed that he should be there, playing with Homer, asking questions at the dinner table, tagging at Luke's heels in the barn.

"Even considering this feels so selfish," he admitted, pressing his lips to her hair.

"I know. Don't you think I've felt it, too? But you deserve a chance at happiness, Luke. We both do. And I'll be beside you every step of the way. If you'll let me."

"You aren't afraid?"

"Of course I'm afraid. But you healed me, Luke. You made me see I still believed in love. In marriage. I want to grow old with you. And if that isn't possible...I'll take whatever time God gives us."

She was right. He knew if he'd asked his parents, they would have said the same thing even had they known how their lives would be cut short. They had loved each other with a steadfastness that had been beautiful. Cait had found Joe and Liz had found Paul. Their relationships hadn't always been easy. And neither was his with Emily. But he loved her. He wanted to spend his life with her. And if he were ever going to be selfish in his life, he figured he might as well make it count.

"What about school? Your job? I know your independence is important to you. I would never want to take that away from you, Em. Don't get me wrong. I want to love you and provide for you and protect you. But I also want you to be your own person. To be happy. Whatever you want to do, the choice is ultimately yours."

He knelt on one knee on the porch, clasping her hand in

his. "So will you marry me, Emily? Marry me and let me be a father to Sam and bring a family home to this ranch?"

Her bottom lip wobbled and he squeezed her fingers. "Everything else we'll figure out as we go along. I will spend every moment making sure you don't regret it. No one will love you harder than me, Em."

"Oh, Lord, I know that!" She knelt in front of him, pressing her palm to his.

"Do you mean it? Really mean it?"

He nodded. "Every word. Marry me, Emily." He smiled. The weight that he'd carried for nearly as long as he could remember lifted. He pulled her close and kissed her, tasting lipstick and tears.

She nodded as he drew back and touched her lips with his thumb.

The phone rang and Luke knew they were running late. But for once his family would have to wait. He let it ring, waiting for Emily's answer.

"Yes, I'll marry you," she whispered, and then her smile blossomed. "As soon as it can be arranged."

EPILOGUE

THE DRIZZLY AUTUMN day couldn't dampen the celebratory mood as the Evans extended family exited the church. First Liz and her brood, dressed all in pink. Then Joe, holding a squirming Janna in his arms and Cait with a hand over her slightly rounded belly. Emily's parents, beaming with pride and squiring a handsome Sam in a new suit between them. And finally, Luke and Emily, grinning from ear to ear. Baby Elina was nestled in Emily's arm, the heirloom Evans christening gown draped over Emily's wrist.

Back at the farm Emily, Liz and Cait laid out food buffet style. Once the kids had filled their plates, the adults followed while Elina was changed into a frilly pink dress and passed between grandparents, aunts and uncles.

Emily and Luke stole a private moment in the kitchen while Liz and Cait flipped through the family albums, the music from the old stereo creating a joyful noise throughout the house.

"Happy anniversary," Emily whispered.

"I first kissed you in this very spot. Do you remember?" Luke pressed his forehead to hers and Emily closed her eyes, wondering how on earth she'd ended up so blissfully happy.

"You cursed before you did it, you know. You were reluctant about everything…"

"Then I am a very lucky man that you persevered."

"I knew a good thing when I saw it."

"I love you, Emily. And our children."

Today the minister had performed two baptisms. Not just baby Elina in her silk-and-lace gown, but also Sam, who hadn't been baptized as a baby. Today Luke had claimed both children, even though the adoption of Sam had gone through months earlier.

"I love you, too. Are you ever going to kiss me though? We're sure to be interrupted at any moment."

He was laughing as he pressed his lips to hers, holding her close. She gave back equally, twining her arms around his neck and standing on tiptoe.

"Hey, Dad, can I change out of this suit and show the girls the new kittens?"

Sam's voice announced his arrival in the kitchen and Luke muttered a light curse as Emily laughed and loosened her arms.

"Oh. Yuck," Sam said.

"Yes, go change," Luke said. "And be smart. We'll both get in trouble if the twins get their dresses dirty."

"Yes, sir."

The swinging door flapped shut as Sam ran out.

"He called me Dad." There was a note of wonder in Luke's voice and Emily smiled.

"Em…when I think of all you've given me…I never would have had the courage to take the test if it hadn't been for you. Suddenly I had more to gain than I had to lose."

"And was it worth it?"

"You'd better believe it," he replied confidently. "I never thought I'd have this. Never thought I'd have love, and a family of my own. I know there are no guarantees, even if it did come back negative. I'm going to grab every last drop of happiness I can."

Emily's heart was so full she couldn't hold it all in any

longer. "Hey, Luke, you know how we talked about the big family I always wanted?"

He raised his eyebrows as a slow smile curved up his cheek. "You thinking of trying again?"

She grinned back. "I think it's too late for that," she answered.

He reached out and took her hand. "Oh, Emily."

"Do you suppose we'll break the girl streak this time?" she asked.

"Who cares?" He raised their joined hands and kissed her thumb. "Every day with our family is a gift, and perfect—just the way it is."

JUNE 2011
HARDBACK TITLES

ROMANCE

Passion and the Prince	Penny Jordan
For Duty's Sake	Lucy Monroe
Alessandro's Prize	Helen Bianchin
Mr and Mischief	Kate Hewitt
Wife in the Shadows	Sara Craven
The Brooding Stranger	Maggie Cox
An Inconvenient Obsession	Natasha Tate
The Girl He Never Noticed	Lindsay Armstrong
The Privileged and the Damned	Kimberly Lang
The Big Bad Boss	Susan Stephens
Her Desert Prince	Rebecca Winters
A Family for the Rugged Rancher	Donna Alward
The Boss's Surprise Son	Teresa Carpenter
Soldier on Her Doorstep	Soraya Lane
Ordinary Girl in a Tiara	Jessica Hart
Tempted by Trouble	Liz Fielding
Flirting with the Society Doctor	Janice Lynn
When One Night Isn't Enough	Wendy S Marcus

HISTORICAL

Ravished by the Rake	Louise Allen
The Rake of Hollowhurst Castle	Elizabeth Beacon
Bought for the Harem	Anne Herries
Slave Princess	Juliet Landon

MEDICAL™

Melting the Argentine Doctor's Heart	Meredith Webber
Small Town Marriage Miracle	Jennifer Taylor
St Piran's: Prince on the Children's Ward	Sarah Morgan
Harry St Clair: Rogue or Doctor?	Fiona McArthur

05011 Gen Std LP

JUNE 2011
LARGE PRINT TITLES

ROMANCE

Flora's Defiance	Lynne Graham
The Reluctant Duke	Carole Mortimer
The Wedding Charade	Melanie Milburne
The Devil Wears Kolovsky	Carol Marinelli
The Nanny and the CEO	Rebecca Winters
Friends to Forever	Nikki Logan
Three Weddings and a Baby	Fiona Harper
The Last Summer of Being Single	Nina Harrington

HISTORICAL

Lady Arabella's Scandalous Marriage	Carole Mortimer
Dangerous Lord, Seductive Miss	Mary Brendan
Bound to the Barbarian	Carol Townend
The Shy Duchess	Amanda McCabe

MEDICAL™

St Piran's: The Wedding of The Year	Caroline Anderson
St Piran's: Rescuing Pregnant Cinderella	Carol Marinelli
A Christmas Knight	Kate Hardy
The Nurse Who Saved Christmas	Janice Lynn
The Midwife's Christmas Miracle	Jennifer Taylor
The Doctor's Society Sweetheart	Lucy Clark

JULY 2011
HARDBACK TITLES

ROMANCE

The Marriage Betrayal	Lynne Graham
The Ice Prince	Sandra Marton
Doukakis's Apprentice	Sarah Morgan
Surrender to the Past	Carole Mortimer
Heart of the Desert	Carol Marinelli
Reckless Night in Rio	Jennie Lucas
Her Impossible Boss	Cathy Williams
The Replacement Wife	Caitlin Crews
Dating and Other Dangers	Natalie Anderson
The S Before Ex	Mira Lyn Kelly
Her Outback Commander	Margaret Way
A Kiss to Seal the Deal	Nikki Logan
Baby on the Ranch	Susan Meier
The Army Ranger's Return	Soraya Lane
Girl in a Vintage Dress	Nicola Marsh
Rapunzel in New York	Nikki Logan
The Doctor & the Runaway Heiress	Marion Lennox
The Surgeon She Never Forgot	Melanie Milburne

HISTORICAL

Seduced by the Scoundrel	Louise Allen
Unmasking the Duke's Mistress	Margaret McPhee
To Catch a Husband…	Sarah Mallory
The Highlander's Redemption	Marguerite Kaye

MEDICAL™

The Playboy of Harley Street	Anne Fraser
Doctor on the Red Carpet	Anne Fraser
Just One Last Night…	Amy Andrews
Suddenly Single Sophie	Leonie Knight

JULY 2011
LARGE PRINT TITLES

ROMANCE

A Stormy Spanish Summer	Penny Jordan
Taming the Last St Claire	Carole Mortimer
Not a Marrying Man	Miranda Lee
The Far Side of Paradise	Robyn Donald
The Baby Swap Miracle	Caroline Anderson
Expecting Royal Twins!	Melissa McClone
To Dance with a Prince	Cara Colter
Molly Cooper's Dream Date	Barbara Hannay

HISTORICAL

Lady Folbroke's Delicious Deception	Christine Merrill
Breaking the Governess's Rules	Michelle Styles
Her Dark and Dangerous Lord	Anne Herries
How To Marry a Rake	Deb Marlowe

MEDICAL™

Sheikh, Children's Doctor...Husband	Meredith Webber
Six-Week Marriage Miracle	Jessica Matthews
Rescued by the Dreamy Doc	Amy Andrews
Navy Officer to Family Man	Emily Forbes
St Piran's: Italian Surgeon, Forbidden Bride	Margaret McDonagh
The Baby Who Stole the Doctor's Heart	Dianne Drake